9:13

Carl Garrett

Published by Carl Garrett

Copyright © 2016 Carl Garrett
All rights reserved.

Cover model: Brandy Mason
Cover photography: Jarod Kearney
Cover design: Lieu Pham, Covertopia.com
eBook formatting: Guido Henkel

This is a work of fiction. Names, characters, places and incidents either are products of the author's imagination or are used fictitiously. Any resemblance to actual events or locales or persons, living or dead, is entirely coincidental. All rights reserved. No part of this publication may be reproduced, distributed or transmitted in any form or by any means, including photocopying, recording, or other electronic or mechanical methods, without the prior written permission of the publisher, except in the case of brief quotations embodied in critical reviews and certain other noncommercial uses permitted by copyright law.

ISBN: 1546400001
ISBN-13: 978-1546400004

To Cindy. Thank you, my love, for being my number one fan.

CONTENTS

1	Prologue: The Night Before	1
2	The First Day	3
3	The Second Day	30
4	The Third Day	58
5	The Fourth Day	83
6	The Fifth Day	105
7	The Sixth Day	144
8	The Last Day	183
9	Epilogue	206
10	Acknowledgements	208
11	About the Author	210

PROLOGUE: THE NIGHT BEFORE

I'm going to die.
The girl wept, and prayed, and waited.
She tapped the screen of her smartphone, squinting in the sudden gleam of light, the only source of illumination in the room. The phone's clock read: 9:10. She'd been crying all day, especially since Andy had told her off and killed her one last shred of hope, but she half-sobbed at the sight just the same.

She knelt, heedless of the filthy concrete floor. The dirt being ground into her boutique jeans was a perfect match with the $200 hairstyle that now hung in greasy strands about her head and the high-end makeup that ran in streaks down her face. All the things that had made her so powerful, now so meaningless.

I'm going to die.
The phone's screen blinked off. The basement had one window, but outside it was night, and the darkness of the room wrapped oppressively around her. She whimpered in panic and tapped the screen again. The screen stayed on this time, the small island of light casting unreal shadows on an old, unlit wood stove, some nearby shelving, and nothing more.

She began, again, to pray the only prayer she knew.

"Our Father, who art in heaven…"

Sweat trickled down her face and soaked her clothing; it was hot down here, the air heavy and thick.

"Hallowed be… be thy name…"

The screen now: 9:11.

"Thy kingdom come, thy will be done, on earth as it is in… in heaven…"

She picked up speed, her voice twisting in panic.

"Give us the day our daily bread, and forgive us our… our trespasses as we forgive those who, who trespass against us. As we forgive…"

9:12. Her sobs began again.

"And lead us not into temptation, but deliver us… de-deliver us from evil, for thine is the kingdom, and the glory, forever and ever…"

9:13.

"Amen." She curled into herself and waited for the end.

For one precious moment there was nothing, the stillness of the room broken only by her own hitching breaths. For that moment, against all her better sense, she allowed herself to hope.

Then she heard it. The cold, dead whisper in the dark.

"Are you sorry?"

THE FIRST DAY

Natasha Briggs always woke before the gun went off.

She bolted from sleep with a sound between a scream and a sob, thrashed free of the sheets and blanket that ensnared her, rolled into a defensive crouch with expert agility. Ready, this time.

Ready for nothing. A small room. A mattress on the bare floor. Unfamiliar creaks and smells. The dream was gone and the quiet house mocked her.

She wept.

She was starting her second cup of coffee when her smartphone, parked on the nearby counter, began to warble.

"Fuck."

Rising from the couch suddenly seemed to take twice the usual effort as she tossed a picked-at croissant onto the coffee table. She grabbed the phone, looked at the screen. It read: LINC.

"Fuck!"

She squelched the idea of tossing the phone in the trash, and answered. "My first day's not 'til Monday, if you remember."

"You need to get out here." The voice on the other end was male and, at the moment, all business. She knew that tone well and didn't question it.

"Where's here?"

"Sixteen-eighty Williamson Road. One six eight zero. Just past Henriksen's."

"Who the hell is Henriksen?"

"The tractor dealership. Don't eat breakfast."

"Why shouldn't I—" BEEP. The call ended. She set down the phone and felt the tightening in her chest that was now too familiar.

Time to go to work.

It wouldn't have been any easier on Monday, she knew that, but she suddenly wanted to cling to the last 48 hours of her unwanted time off, like a kid the day before the start of school. She noticed her breaths coming faster and shallower, and forced them to slow.

Breathe in on four, out on eight. Just like Benson showed you.

She stood and moved past furniture haphazardly placed by the movers, past unopened boxes that would stay unopened for now. She grabbed the blazer she'd worn the day before off the back of a chair, moved down the hall of the small rental house to the bedroom, where she rummaged through another box to find a shirt and slacks. Morning sunlight streamed through the bedroom window, which treated her to a view of a scraggly field, a neighbor's house barely visible in the distance.

She glanced into the mirror she had perched precariously atop the dresser. The woman who looked back at her was in her thirties, with a wiry build and unruly brunette hair. From certain angles she might be considered pretty. Her clothes were urban, sharp-cut and expensive, but today they looked like they were meant for someone else.

From the top dresser drawer, she gathered her badge in its leather wallet, her gun and holster, and a prescription

9:13

pill bottle. She popped open the bottle and dry-swallowed a pill. The woman in the mirror scowled at her with contempt.

She hadn't yet been issued a department car, so she drove her truck to the scene.

Her eyes half on the road, she rummaged in the glove compartment, grabbed a packet of granola bars from her stash. With a practiced flourish, she tore the cellophane wrapper open with her teeth and munched. Surrounded by the familiar shimmies and smells of her truck, the bland crunch of the granola, she could almost imagine she was still in the city, on her way to start her shift at the job that had once been her life's dream.

One look out the windshield was enough to bring her back to reality.

The town was old. The section she drove through now was a few blocks off the tiny, shiny main street strip. The houses were small and poor, like stunted trees somehow, and most of them had peeling paint and unkept lawns. Wright's Crossing, the county seat of Colvin County, Virginia, was an isolated crossroads town surrounded by hours of flat, scrubby country in every direction. Its glory days of tobacco and railroads were nearly a hundred years gone, and it was now populated by the descendants of the people who had been too dumb to leave.

Don't think about where you are. If you think about it, you'll go crazy.

She almost missed the turn onto the street that took her out of the main part of town, passed a shabby tractor store and buy-here-pay-here car lot that were right across from a gleaming new library. And then, almost instantly, the road went from smooth asphalt to chintzy tar-and-chip, and she was surrounded by trees on either side.

Last night, Linc had told her over beers, "We were an independent city for like, two hundred years almost, no shit," knocking back his beer in that way he had of taking a swig and turning it into a glug. "City council reverted it to a town after the last cigarette factory closed in '98."

"So what's the difference between a city and a town?" She only sipped her beer. They had not had a drink together in years, and she didn't want both of them to be drunk at the same time.

"Means the county has to pay for services."

"But they kept the town police force?"

He had shrugged. "People didn't want to give it up. County sheriff's a joke." After another swig/glug, he had said, "Doesn't matter, it's all lost kittens and stolen lawnmowers around here. You won't know what to do with yourself, girl." He had smiled that classic schoolboy smile of his and she had tried not to notice.

She noticed Williamson Road too late, swore as she screeched the truck to a stop and backed up to make the turn.

The house was easy to spot, its long gravel driveway crowded with a fire engine, two black-and-whites, and several other cars, with a uniformed officer guarding the entrance to the driveway. As she slowed to make the turn, a clean-cut man, looked like he was in his late twenties, waved her down from the other side of the road. His camera and digital recorder gave him away as a reporter almost as much as his disingenuous smile.

"Morning. Chad Merriman from the *Times*, can you tell me what's happening?"

She gave him the glacial look she'd perfected for dealing with the press. "I thought the *Colvin County Times* folded two years ago."

He faltered, but only for a moment. "We're online-only now. Kind of like *Times* two-point-oh." He wasn't local; he spoke without a trace of a southern accent.

The officer across the road called out, "Piss off,

Merriman."

Unfazed, the young man asked, "You the new detective?"

She replied, "Piss off, Merriman," and juiced the engine, just to make him jump.

She turned in to face the house.

It was a weatherworn country saltbox, with a sagging porch roof and boarded-up windows. She parked fifty yards away, next to what was likely the CSI van, but could still make out faded, peeling paint. Ivy covered almost the entire left side, and the yard was a jungle, the grass a three-foot-high tangle that would need a machete instead of a mower. It was a dead thing, waiting patiently for nature to pull it back into the hungering earth.

She suddenly felt the familiar clenching in her chest, the shortening of her breaths.

It would have to be a place like that, wouldn't it. My first day, the first case. Goddamn it.

She went through Benson's breathing exercises again. *In on four, out on eight, in on four, out on eight.* But impatience nagged at her. They were waiting, watching the new detective.

You've got this, Briggs. Come on, you've got this.

She popped a second pill as she slid out of the truck into the sweltering Virginia summer.

There was a small klatch of people confabbing next to the fire engine, four firefighters and a cop. As she got closer, their conversation, all sports and right-wing politics from what she could hear, subsided. The cop turned toward her as he took a drag from the stub of a cigarette. He was a heavy-set man who looked to be in his forties, and his pudgy, florid face broke into a scowl. "Help you, Miss?" His badge read, "P. Dudley," and he damn well knew who she was.

"Officer Dudley. I'm Detective Briggs."

He regarded her with thinly-veiled contempt, making a show of grinding the cigarette under his heel before responding. "So, you're Linc's girl, huh?" His snaky eyes glittered. "Thought he liked 'em with a little more chest." The firefighters smirked.

Keeping her voice even and professional, she replied, "You must be the one in charge of securing the scene outside the house, Officer Dudley."

He snorted, "Yeah, what about it?"

She leaned in, smiled just a little sweetly as she said, "Then you might want to pick up that cigarette butt before someone runs DNA on it and nails you as a suspect."

Dudley's face turned a deeper, angry red. She kept her face close to his as she followed with, "And it's Detective Briggs, Officer Dudley, if that's not too much for you." The firefighters tried to smother their mirth and failed.

From behind she heard, "Glad you could make it."

She turned.

Detective Lincoln Meyers was the same age as she, muscular but a little paunchy, his broad jock build now softened since his days in Richmond PD. His features were unremarkable, but his eyes were deep. They had always been his best feature.

Linc asked, "Your GPS take you the long way around?"

She fell into step beside him as he turned toward the house. "Next time you can give me a little more than 'past Henriksen's'."

He shrugged by way of an answer. "You met Dudley, huh."

"'Linc's girl'? Really?"

"You knew it was gonna happen. Besides, Dudley's the one who lost out to you for the job."

Her brows arched in surprise. "McGann had an applicant on the inside?"

"Yeah."

"And passed him over for me?"

"He's a waste and McGann's got enough of those. Me included." He smiled. For a moment, she smiled back.

The house loomed closer. She clung to the familiar

feelings of the cop routine, the sound of Linc's voice, trying to keep a handle on her accelerating heartbeat. "Is this place even in our jurisdiction?"

"Just. Town limit's about a mile down the road. Lucky fuckin' us."

For the moment, she could think of nothing else to ask. Her shoulders felt the heat as the dark fabric of her jacket absorbed the strong sun. They reached the driveway cul-de-sac.

She noticed the man first. He looked to be in his late thirties and had the weathered features of a country boy beneath a pair of glasses with cheap plastic rims. He was tall, thin but muscular in the way of working men. He wore a polo shirt with "CSI" emblazoned on the breast pocket. He seemed strangely lost in thought, staring at a car parked in front of the house, a slick, late-model import. "A four-series," Natasha remarked. "Not cheap."

The man jumped a little, but recovered. "Only 'bout forty grand or so. The M6's almost three times that." He held out his hand. "Eddie Shifflett. I'm the CSI. You must be Miss Briggs?"

"Detective Briggs, yes." Eddie Shifflett had a firm handshake, but his eyes were restless and could not hold her gaze for long.

"Oh. Detective Briggs. Sorry."

She motioned toward the car. "Belong to someone you know?"

"No. Just a... car freak, that's me. Finished taking pictures, now we're just waitin' on the warrant." He ambled off toward the van.

From behind her, Linc said, "Car's registered to Denise Randolph."

She studied the car to avoid looking at the house. "Is that the Randolphs who own Virginia Meats?"

Linc nodded. "Slaughterhouse is the biggest employer in town. Her dad's Gerald Randolph, the state senator."

She mused, "It's a two-hour drive to the nearest

Beemer dealership. Safe to say Denise has money and wants people to know it?"

"You don't miss a trick. You'll learn all about the Randolphs by the time we're done. Housekeeper says Denise is out of town on business, but she's got a daughter who's sixteen. Housekeeper doesn't know where she is."

She could see little through the car windows beyond a high-end purse tossed haphazardly in the passenger footwell. *Time to move on.* "Can I talk to the responding officer?"

"What, you don't trust me?" She didn't answer, cast her eyes to the ground. He shook his head in amused exasperation. "Same old Nat." He waved over a tall, grim patrolwoman. "Natasha Briggs, Liz Paxton."

Natasha felt an iron grip as they shook hands and exchanged pleasantries, but the woman's face was drawn and pale. "Officer Paxton. What can you tell me?"

"Terrible," the woman said in a soft voice. "I've seen farm accidents weren't this bad."

Natasha remained silent. *Wait for it.*

Finally, the woman resumed. "Neighbor saw the smoke when she was driving to work, called the fire department. Fire was in the basement, but it hadn't spread. I think they said it was just the ceiling tiles that were burning. But anyway, when they got down there and found it, they called us."

Natasha frowned. "Christ, I'll bet the scene is a mess."

Paxton nodded. "Sure is." She went on to describe the check she'd made of the rest of the house, as per procedure, and finding no one else, she'd sealed the scene until the warrant could be obtained.

Natasha made herself look at the house. Up close, the signs of neglect and decay were even more evident. The gutters were rusted and skewed, and a thin layer of green lichen covered much of the porch floor. "Have we talked to the owner?"

9:13

Linc looked thoughtful as his gaze followed hers. "Owner died about two years ago. No, more like a year and a half. They can't find any heirs. County's about to seize it for taxes."

Something about his expression made her ask, "Did you know the owner?"

He hesitated for a moment, but replied, "No."

She might have pressed him further, but the crackle of tires on gravel caught her attention. A county-issued sedan stopped at the end of the line of vehicles, and she recognized the man driving it. Linc whispered, "Look busy."

She quipped, "I just have to look busier than you." But she found herself sweating from more than just the heat. As Linc walked away to greet the car and its occupant, Paxton asked casually, "So, you and Meyers used to work together?"

"We drove a patrol car together in Richmond."

"Guess you two got some history."

Natasha carefully replied, "Yeah. Guess we do."

McGann. A hard-eyed brick of a man, his hair still iron-black despite his age of fifty-five, he approached the house with athletic strides, and without ceremony handed a piece of paper to Linc. When he asked, "Talked to the Randolphs?" his voice spoke of a man with a military background, a fact that Natasha, who had researched her new boss carefully, already knew.

"Left messages for her and the old man." Linc nodded to the firefighters, who cranked up a large generator and readied a number of utility lights. Eddie appeared with his kit.

Over the clamor of the generator, McGann scrutinzed Linc. "You ready for this?"

Linc's voice was steady and strong as he replied, "Yes, sir," but his face was that of a kid called to the front of the class.

McGann's glare was not encouraging. "Update me

before lunch." He turned toward Natasha, seemingly as an afterthought. "Looks like you got here just in time, Briggs." Before she could reply, he strode back to his car and in a few moments had backed onto the road and turned toward town.

Natasha watched the car disappear. "He always that way?"

Linc exhaled. "Nah. Sometimes he's cranky."

The front door squawked as it opened. The firefighters entered, their boots tromp-squeaking on the dry boards of the porch as they carried the lights inside. Natasha noticed Eddie, Paxton, and another uniform lining up behind them.

Linc proffered a box of nitrile gloves. She shook her head, pulling some of her preferred brand from her pocket. Linc shook his head, grinned as she snapped them on. But as he faced the open door at the front of the line, Natasha could see the telltale tremor in his hands, just like he'd had before every traffic stop in the old days. Linc exhaled into his game face, and stepped through the door. "Showtime."

The gloom of the place wrapped around her like a shroud. Beyond the expected smell of smoke and char was one of dust, of mold and emptiness and decay. Her pulse began to quicken again, and she could feel the air getting stuck in her lungs. *It's not the same house.* She forced herself to observe the minute details around her. *It's not the same house. Doesn't smell the same. The sun is shining outside. You're not in that place. You're safe. You're safe.*

She had stepped into a small foyer, with a staircase to the right leading upstairs and a hallway to the left. The house seemed to suck up the sunlight before it could get a foot past the front door. She could just make out a pass-through to what had to be the living room on the left.

She heard Linc say, "Just one up here, for now. There." The glare of the utility light blinded her for a moment as firefighters wrangled it into place at the end of the short hall, illuminating a closed door at the end (kitchen, had to be) and an open door to the right.

She said, "We should set up a second one in the living room," and it wasn't until she noticed the fish-eye from Paxton and the other uniform that she realized her faux pas. *Christ Briggs, let him be in charge.*

Linc himself just shrugged. "Sure." He clicked on a formidable cop flashlight as he led her through the open door to the right, and she followed, pulling from her pocket the tiny LED light that was all she had at the moment.

The door opened onto a set of wooden stairs. The smokey, charred smell intensified, and the stairs sagged under their weight. She let him get two steps ahead, following carefully as her small halo of light flicked from stair to stair. The staircase ended with a sharp turn to the left, and they were in the basement.

One tiny window, set high up, almost to the ceiling, allowed a small sprat of sunlight to enter. The light splayed across a bare cinder block wall, a wood stove, an old analog clock. They stood off to the side until the utility lights were set up. When they were turned on, she gazed upon a nightmare scene caught between the harsh glow of the lights and the pitch-black shadows they couldn't reach. Linc grumbled, "What a fuckin' mess."

The basement was a rough concrete box. It was smaller than the rest of the home's floorplan. As she'd expected, the above-ground kitchen and indoor plumbing had come after the original house was built. Shelving units were visible on the outskirts of the light. Every visible surface glistened with wet. A portion of the ceiling had been torn out and the hole doused by the firefighters. Scorched pieces of drywall and insulation littered the floor. The ceiling no doubt had caught fire from the object that now lay under a dripping tarp.

As she heard the clomping of the firefighters going back up the stairs, she studied the burnt hole in the ceiling.

"It's a wonder the whole house didn't go up."

"The tiles probably have asbestos 'cause of the wood stove."

She heard new footsteps on the stairs, lighter this time, as Eddie descended with his kit. Addressing Linc, he asked, "Pictures first?" Eddie's face seemed pale, his expression hesitant, but it could have just been the light.

"Yeah." Linc carefully grabbed a side of the tarp, and lifted it aside.

They stared at the object beneath.

Natasha's breath caught. "What happened to stolen lawnmowers and lost puppies?"

Linc gulped. "Guess I lied."

The corpse lay on its side, curled almost into a fetal position. Most of it was charred black, the head, arms, most of the torso completely consumed. The fire seemed to have tapered off as it went down the legs, for below the knees they were almost untouched, the perfectly white skin only adding to the grotesque horror of the sight. Natasha detected the campfire smell of a burned human body, the burnt-tire reek of scorched hair. She could taste it in the back of her throat. She pulled a small bottle of eucalyptus oil from a pocket, dabbing some under her nose.

Watching her, Linc asked, "Why not just the vapor rub stuff?"

"Cause it opens the nasal passages more. Didn't you read last month's issue of *Police*?" His reply was a roll of the eyes.

The flash of Eddie's camera lit up the scene with a momentary brilliance, bringing every detail of the terrible sight into keen-edged relief. She steadied her breathing. *In on four, out on eight.* But she felt her mind begin to sharpen amid the macabre illumination provided by the utility lights and Eddie's flash, her breathing finding its rhythm. "Definitely looks like a liquid accelerant." She sniffed. "Gasoline?"

"Yeah."

"And a vertical pour pattern."

"Yeah."

She held out her hand; he didn't need to ask, handing her his flashlight. "You never should have given up your duty belt."

"Made me look fat."

"Wasn't the belt."

"Fuck you."

She played the powerful light around, found what she was looking for almost immediately – the blackened, twisted remains of a plastic gas can. Linc said, "Firefighters must have kicked it over there without noticing."

She reflected. "Or the perp tossed it there after lighting her up." He looked annoyed. If they were following their old pattern, which so far they were, he'd now start getting huffy if she didn't agree with him.

The water on the floor sparkled in bizarre patterns as Eddie's camera flashed. Natasha coughed. The air was becoming a fusty soup, the water evaporating and mingling with the mildew and dust. "You said Denise Randolph had a teenage daughter?"

"Yeah. Name's Grace."

She crouched, regarded the unblemished feet. "The sandals look a little wild for a mom who drives a Beemer, not to mention the nail polish color."

From behind, she heard a sound escape Eddie, something between a gasp and a sob.

She rose and turned to him. In the glare of the utility lights, Eddie seemed to have shrunk, his face distorted and unnatural. In her best gentle-cop voice, she said "You knew her." It wasn't a question. Questions were easier to deny.

Eddie shook his head. His voice cracked as he replied, "I didn't know her, like. It's just a shame. Dyin' so young. Like that."

From behind her, Linc said, "Take five, Eddie."

"Sure. Thanks." Eddie retreated and sat down heavily on one of the stairs.

Linc hadn't moved. She watched as he stared at the body, holding his almost-bare notepad in front of him like a shield. The thought blinked into her mind with perfect clarity before she could stop it. *He's not up to this. He's the primary, and he's not up to this.*

She knew what she had to do. She gingerly rounded the corpse and crouched down on the other side. Linc followed her lead. One blackened hand was clutched to the chest. She looked intently in its general direction. Linc followed again, his eyes searching along with hers. She waited. She shifted her weight, willing him to notice what she had noticed. Then she gave up and asked, "Something in the hand?"

Linc's expression was one of relief and irritation as he carefully rubbed at an object clutched in the shriveled hand, revealing a metallic glint. "A phone. Holy shit. Eddie, take a shot of this." In a moment, Eddie's camera flashed in reply. To Natasha he said, "Good catch," and she suddenly felt almost like blushing.

He was quicker on the uptake when she stepped back to inspect the shelving units and he noticed, almost immediately, "They're all crowded together, like someone pushed them away to make room up front."

"But it happened a long time ago. The scrape marks aren't fresh." She looked toward the sound of footsteps on the stairs. Paxton entered the basement, and Linc did an unwieldy dance around the corpse, the debris, and Eddie to greet her.

Natasha shined the flashlight amid the dusty shelves. They were crammed full, but organized with exquisite precision. Jars of nails and screws were arranged in ascending order, not only according to the size of the nails and screws but by the size of the jars, as well. Board games, still in their original, now-faded boxes, were stacked atop each other with the edges perfectly flush;

even the tape around the torn box corners was exacting. But the dust covering this area was undisturbed. She moved back toward the body.

His camera put away, Eddie inspected the corpse's other hand, outstretched plaintively across the floor. She asked, "Any chance for fingerprints?"

"Doubt it. Maybe, after I soak 'em. Dental should be good, though." He twitched as he worked, edgy and apprehensive. She left him to it. Paxton and Linc stood at the foot of the stairs, Paxton holding the purse they'd seen inside the Beemer, but her tone of voice became low and conspiratorial as Natasha approached, Paxton's shoulder subtly curving to exclude her. She decided not to press her luck and moved on.

With the utility lights focused on the body, the space beside the wood stove extending along the wall to the corner was in shadow. She played her light across the stove and then the clock, which was stopped just after nine o'clock. She crouched to inspect the floor and found nothing but more water and blackened drywall bits. She realized that water and schmutz had soaked into her shoes, and cursed. Something on the wall glinted in the beam of the flashlight, a metal ring, actually a large eye screw, fixed into the wall about four feet from the floor. *Nothing here. Move on.*

She stood, slapping a blotch of dust from her slacks.

It was then that she felt it.

It started as a faint sensation, a tingle along the back of her neck, goosebumps on her arm, a prickly presence that seemed to be all around her, touching her, not a random sensation but something more deliberate. It seemed to reach inside her, *through* her, and for a moment she felt a horrifying *something*, a presence and mind that was not her own, as it touched and tested her.

She thought she heard a voice, a whisper, wafting in and out of the periphery of her hearing. She thought she caught the word, *"Sssoorrrry…"* but then it was gone and

Linc was asking, "What'd you find?"

She blinked. He was standing over her, inspecting the ring in the wall illuminated by her flashlight, and she felt a surge of irritation and embarrassment as she wondered how long she'd been standing there. "Nothing." She rose. "What was in the purse?"

"Grace Randolph's ID, to start."

Shit. It wasn't the first dead teenage girl she'd ever dealt with, but it was a hell of a way to start a new job. Linc asked, "Anything else you want to see here? I figured we'd do the rest of the house and leave Eddie to it."

From behind, Eddie: "Yeah, old Dee-tective Meyers don't want to get his feet wet no more."

Linc smirked. "Privileges of rank, Shifflett. Paxton can keep you company."

Paxton nodded, but she didn't join in the ribbing, and Natasha made note of it.

As she mounted the steps, Natasha took one more look at the hellish tableau below her. A thought suddenly struck her and she stopped. "Look at how she held the phone."

Linc couldn't check his momentum in time to keep from bumping into her, and she didn't mind. "Huh?"

"Look how she clutched it to her chest, protected it."

Linc winced. "Jesus."

Eddie looked up from opening his fingerprint kit. "What's that mean?"

She stayed silent to let Linc have the moment. "It means," he said, grim, "that she was probably still alive when she was set on fire."

Eddie threw up.

Surveying the living room, she and Linc beheld a disaster area of empty bottles and cans, cigarette butts, fast food wrappers, and run-down furniture. Graffiti covered the walls. An empty propane lantern lay amid the clutter.

9:13

Linc grumbled, "Witness says that kids break in here to party. Never bothered calling us about it, of course. Probably a hundred different prints, none of them'll be the perp. What do you think?"

"I think I'm glad you're the primary."

"Feelin' the love, here."

She smiled. "Maybe Eddie will get some prints from the basement."

"I ain't holding my breath."

The kitchen was in a similar state, with smashed dishes littering the floor and "All Niggers Must Die" spray-painted across the wall. She checked the overflowing trash can in case the perp, if there was one, had tossed anything on his way out; it was amazing how force of habit got people in trouble like that.

Linc, standing behind her, said, "Christ, is that a diaper in there?"

"Yeah."

He muttered, "Trash," and she knew he wasn't talking about the contents of the can.

She changed the subject. "Check the upstairs?"

"Right behind you."

She carried a powerful hand-lantern they'd borrowed off the firefighters. It was her only source of light as they ascended the staircase to the second floor, and it gave Natasha a surreal feeling, as if by releasing her grip on its handle she would disappear and be absorbed by the gloom. The air, already stifling, got hotter and staler.

The bathroom happened to be the first door they came to. Linc said, "You got to be kidding me." He almost gagged.

The partiers had been conscientious enough to not do their business on the living room floor (at least mostly, based on the smell), but not smart enough or sober enough to realize that the plumbing didn't work. In one corner lay a tumble of bunched-up burger wrappers that had been pressed into service as toilet paper. The mess that had piled up in the toilet bowl was unspeakable. She took out the bottle of eucalyptus oil and gave her nose another dab.

Outside in the hallway, Linc said, "Gimme some of that."

Aside from the awful conditions in and around the toilet, there was not much else to see. She noted that the bathroom was painted a loud shade of blue, unlike the standard white that covered every other wall she'd seen. A decorative switch plate covered the light switch by the door; it was in the shape of the cross, with the message, "Jesus is the ONLY salvation!" stamped into it in bas relief. She stepped back into the hallway. "Want to take a look?"

"I trust you."

"Pussy."

"Meow."

The master bedroom was next. One of the boards covering a nearby window had come loose, and a stab of sunlight illuminated the room. The air circulating through the broken panes did little to help the stuffy heat. *Christ, I need a shower.* Her shirt was sodden with sweat, and she detested the clammy feeling against her skin.

There was a dresser with most of the drawers pulled out and smashed, a single bed covered with a filthy, stained sheet. Natasha remarked, "Owner wasn't married, or at least had no one in his life."

"What?"

"The mattress is like, dorm-sized."

"Huh."

She looked at him. He stood in the middle of the room, his body language tight. His hands went into and out of his pockets.

She asked, "What is it?"

"What's what?"

"Being in this house bothers you."

"Being on this case bothers me. Finding burned-up kids bothers me."

His eyes did not meet hers. He shifted from one foot to another and stared at the wreckage of the dresser. Then he said, "It's my first real case, okay? I wasn't kidding about the lawnmowers and puppies."

She relented. "I'm sorry. I don't know what's wrong with me."

A sly smile. "Wish I had the time to tell you."

Before she could tell him off, Linc's phone warbled. Natasha noticed the word GINA flashing across the screen. Linc sagged, his expression clouding with annoyance. "Can you finish up here?"

"Sure." She gestured with the lantern. "Need me to walk you down?"

He produced his own flashlight. "I'm good."

She listened to his tentative steps receding down the stairway, heard him answer, "Hey, Babe" in his best fake-happy voice, as she opened the final door, across from the bathroom.

The first thing she noticed was the same loud shade of blue on the walls. There was a vanity with a cracked mirror, a small bed with a well-worn mattress. The air here felt especially close.

She opened and closed the intact vanity drawers. They were empty. On the wall over the vanity, the word "Crystal" had been drawn in large, awkward lettering, using what looked like a black marker. *So the owner had a kid, a girl, teenage or close to it.*

The bed was shoved into the corner farthest from the door. She knelt down and shined the light under the bed, finding a filthy t-shirt and a filthier pair of panties. On a whim, she raised the mattress and peeked between it and the box spring, but found nothing.

She exited the room.

And heard the voice again.

"*Sssorrryyy...*" She startled, stood motionless in the murky hallway. She strained to listen.

Jesus Christ, what is this?

"*... you sssorrrry...*" It seemed louder now, not in volume, but somehow its presence in her mind had gotten larger. That feeling, that horrid, invasive sensation she'd felt in the basement returned, like something had seen inside her soul and had not been pleased.

She pressed a hand to her forehead, felt salt-sticky sweat.

Go away.

Whatever the fuck this is, just go away.

It did not.

"*Are you... sssorrry.*" A deep, black dread welled up inside her. This could not happen. Not now. She breathed deep, *in on four, out on eight, in on four, out on eight. Please, God. Please.*

"Nat?"

It was Linc. She reached for his voice and clung to it, held it close as she breathed out the constriction in her chest. She opened her eyes and discovered his hand on her arm. The voice was gone.

"You okay?"

"Yeah. Good." She was grateful that the darkness was hiding the expression on her face.

"Find anything?"

"No. Did your call go okay?"

He replied, "Yeah, fine," and she knew he was lying.

"Does Eddie have any help with combing this place for trace?"

Linc suddenly let out a loud, braying laugh and clapped her on the shoulder. "That'd be us, darlin'. Welcome to the sticks."

"So," Linc, said, "What do you think?"

She blinked in the brightness of the sun. It was getting

late in the day. The outside air was no cooler than it was inside the house, but fresher, free of dust and char. "This my entrance exam, or are you fishing for stuff to tell McGann?"

"You'll never know."

She reflected. "The fingerprints we lifted will lead back to a few local troublemakers who had nothing to do with this. The fact that the purse and wallet were left in the car rules out robbery as motive. Whether or not she was burned alive, the intent was to kill her." She paused. "To *destroy* her."

"What about suicide?"

She noted Dudley's cigarette butt, still twisted into the gravel and dirt as they approached her car. "Rich girls don't kill themselves that way." She added, "We need to get tech working on the phone as soon as possible."

"If by 'tech' you mean Randall, I don't figure he's too busy."

She blushed. "Sorry."

His smile was kind. "It's okay. You'll get used to it."

As they reached her truck, she asked, "You want me to go with you when you notify the mother?"

"McGann already called her." Off her puzzled look, he replied, "It's the Randolphs. Listen, the witness who called in the fire won't be home from work 'til after eight. Can you do the interview?"

"What, is it date night or something?"

"Yeah, kind of, but more than that I like making you do stuff."

"Fine. My day's shot as it is."

He turned to walk back to his car, but stopped and faced her again. "You know, it's okay if you had a moment up there. It happens."

She kept her gaze on the truck's door as she opened it. "Didn't use to."

"And chill out with the 'Detective Briggs' thing." He touched her shoulder. "You're among friends here."

She rolled her eyes. "Yes, Mom." But she let her eyes linger on him a touch longer than she should have as he walked away.

As she pulled the door of the truck closed, fumbling for her keys, she discovered an object on the seat next to her. It was a mason jar, an honest-to-God mason jar, full of an amber-colored liquid. She opened the jar and inhaled a sharp, bready smell. Her face broke into the kind of smile she hadn't felt in a long time. "You've got to be kidding me."

A note was attached, written in Linc's handwriting. It read: "Don't worry, the cousin of a guy I know makes it. Sip it slow unless you're feeling suicidal. Welcome to the sticks."

A small crowd of bystanders milled around the area across the street as she stopped at the driveway's edge. There were housewives taking pictures with their phones, even some with kids in tow. There were a few slackers, a guy in a suit, a washed-out young woman in a long skirt who stood apart from the rest. Natasha noted with interest that there were no television cameras. Merriman was still the only one around who gave her the journalist vibe. Merriman made eye contact from across the road, grinned as he tapped his digital recorder. Mindful of the housewives and their cameras, she avoided giving him even a frown.

She turned left, toward town.

The brain-jazz of the new case began to wear off, and she felt the consequences of going all day on nothing but coffee and anti-anxiety pills. Her stomach ached and her head was a hot brick.

You did good, Briggs. You held it together.

What was it Billy used to say? Hold it together and you hold...

She blinked and discovered that time had fast-forwarded and she had just passed Henriksen's on her way

9:13

back to town.

She realized it was the first thought she'd had about Billy Fletcher in weeks. There was a deep sorrow in her heart, but if honesty were called for she didn't know exactly why. Was it the sudden memory of Billy himself? Or the fact that only six months after his death, she was already forgetting him?

She glared at her reflection in the rearview mirror. *Get some food. Get some rest.*

You have work to do.

Linc watched her truck turn left and head toward town.

"You two worked together, huh?" He almost jumped; since when could Dudley walk up on someone that quietly?

"Drove a squad car together back in Richmond." Which Dudley damn well already knew.

"Guess you two have some history."

Linc carefully replied, "Yeah. Guess we do."

The young woman waited.

The reporter left. Then the gossips. Then the two loafers. For a while it was just her and the man in the suit. She thought at first he must be a pervert, standing there in the sun not making conversation, glancing at her ankles from time to time. *The mind governed by the flesh is death.* A verse from the book of Romans that more people would do well to remember. But in the end, without hardly looking at her, he'd handed her a business card and set off in a gleaming SUV that belched clouds of oil smoke when he accelerated. The card read: Rodney Palmer, Attorney at Law.

It was hot. She retreated to her car to avoid the sun, but the car had no AC. Bake or burn. Time passed. The passersby and the cop at the driveway entrance ignored her, which suited her fine.

Finally, she saw what she'd been waiting for: a tow truck, rolling left onto the road and pulling behind it the small BMW.

She could tell at a glance it was Grace Randolph's car, and the fear that had been building since she arrived blossomed into horror.

Grace Randolph's car, at that house.

Merciful Father, what can it mean?

The witness, Shayla Buchanan, was a doughy, genial woman in her forties who lived dirty. Natasha perched stiffly on the edge of a stained couch and tried not to choke on the cat urine smell that permeated the room. A toddler in a faded "Grammy's Princess!" t-shirt screeched as she chased the cat around the squalid trailer.

"Sorry, she's a handful," said Shayla, "I got custody 'cause my daughter got locked up."

"Oh. Sorry to hear that." A television blared at near-earsplitting volume in the background, but Shayla didn't seem to notice. Natasha struggled to concentrate.

The woman shrugged. "They sent her to jail, didn't send the guy who got her hooked."

"Oh." She waited three seconds, what she had once calculated as the necessary pause before changing the subject. "So, you saw the smoke at—"

"Get you anything?"

"I'm sorry?"

"Somethin' to drink?" The shriek from the other room might have been the toddler or the cat. Natasha didn't wonder why the cat peed everywhere.

"No. Thanks. Could you turn the TV down?"

"Oh, yeah, sorry." There were several remote controls lying about; it took her longer to find the right one than it would have to walk the three feet to the TV. "I was drivin' past the Salyers place on my way to my job at

Riverside. That's actually my second job. I got two of them right now, since I got her to take care of."

"The Salyers place? That's the house where the body was found?"

"That's the house. Man named Salyers lived there. Guess you heard he killed himself."

Natasha looked up. "Really."

"Yeah, he was a cop, too, you know. Worked state police before he came here, is what I heard."

"I see." *One. Two. Three.* "So, you saw the smoke."

"Yeah, was just a little, coming out from a window or something, like the fire just started. I figured it must be one of those punks trying to burn the place down."

She felt an itch prickle on the back of her hand. *If that was a flea I'll burn my fucking clothes.* "You knew about the people partying there?"

"'Course I did."

"Did you ever call the police about it?"

Shayla shrugged and scratched herself. "Wasn't my business."

"Alright." The television show cut to a jittery commercial. "So, you saw the smoke around…"

"Five forty-five or so. I got to be at Riverside by six. They dock you fifteen minutes if you're like, ten seconds late down there."

"Oh." *One. Two. Three.* "Did you see anyone leaving the house? Anyone running away, or a car driving away?"

Shayla was engrossed by the commercial and took a moment to respond. The toddler screamed again. "No, didn't see no one. This road's pretty quiet that time of morning."

Natasha tried a different tack. "Do you know the name of anyone who parties at that house?"

This got Shayla's attention. She turned off the TV and leaned over, lowering her voice in a conspiratorial tone. "There's this guy named Justin. McDaniel's his last name, I think, but I don't know for sure. Used to work the same shift as me, but they fired him for being high on the job. I seen his truck pulling into there once or twice. They all drive around the back of the house and put blankets on the windows, so nobody can see they're there."

Natasha said simply, "His truck." When white trash witnesses were on a roll, you needed to know how to redirect them without interrupting.

"Yeah, it's a big old red truck. It's like, from the eighties, you can tell it's old. He got it when his granddad passed away last year. 'Least that's what he said."

A crash came from another room. The toddler screamed again. Shayla rose and hustled off with a "Sorry, be right back."

Natasha closed her notebook. It was as good a place to stop as any.

She successfully fought the urge to brush herself off as she descended the flimsy metal steps from the trailer. Even in the waning sunlight the air was oppressive with humidity, even worse here in the sticks than when she'd lived in the city. She heard Shayla's voice, scolding, then heard the toddler start to howl.

It was just after nine o'clock as she slid into her truck. She cranked the AC as she backed up to point the truck toward the road. She thought of calling Linc, but remembered what he said about "date night" and thought better of it. Justin, according to Shayla Buchanan, had moved to Newport News a month or so ago. He and his old red truck could wait until morning. She pulled a bottle of diet soda from the truck's cup holder and swigged, wincing at how warm it had gotten in the brief time she'd been inside.

The dashboard clock read: 9:13. She accelerated as fast as she dared down the narrow, rutted driveway. She hadn't taken another pill since her time at the crime scene and felt a small amount of triumph at the thought. She could feel her mind humming with the rush of a new case.

For the first time in many months, she allowed herself

to hope.

Maybe this really will work. Get back in the groove, close a few cases. Maybe this will even

THERE WAS A WOMAN IN THE ROAD!

She screamed, slammed on the brakes, felt the truck momentarily fishtail on the dusty track, jerked against her seatbelt and beheld...

A dog. Scrawny and filthy and lost. It yipped and bounded away.

She fought to calm her breathing, felt her temples buzzing with adrenaline. *It wasn't a dog. It was a woman. It was, I know it.* Her cop brain kicked in. *Young. Late teens. Dirty. Blonde hair. Sleeveless dress – or tank top and skirt. Was she hurt? She was angry. She was thin. Something around her neck, something like...*

A chain?

Behind her, she heard Shayla Buchanan call out, "You okay, Officer?" while the toddler and the TV wailed in the background.

She drank that night, red wine, because although tomorrow's hangover would be a killer, red always gave her the best shot at sleep.

THE SECOND DAY

The tech room was a yard sale of disparate computers and AV equipment, but it was organized and clean. Natasha wouldn't have expected that of Randall, a stubbly, mid-twenties geek who dressed in t-shirts and corduroys. She and Linc stood behind him as he woke his computer monitor from sleep. The smell that wafted from him told her he favored Indian food and didn't bathe every day.

As the computer came to life, Linc remarked, "Dentals confirmed it was Grace Randolph."

Before she could reply, Randall said, "We got smokin' lucky on the data retrieval," as he opened an onscreen folder to reveal several files. Natasha waited for him to laugh at his own pun, but he didn't seem to notice it. The computer beeped and she winced at the sound. Her head was a fiery brick, the hangover as bad as expected.

Linc asked, "We got texts? Emails?"

"Patience, Detective Meyers, this is why you so often lose at poker. I figured you'd want to see the good stuff first."

Natasha perked up through the fog of her hangover. "Video?"

Randall smirked. "Who's a god? Let's hear

everybody say it."

The screen flickered into a herky-jerky image of a high school hallway, panning past scratched lockers and institutional gray walls until the camera found its target. Grace Randolph stood resplendent, poised, flawless, in fashions that were clearly a cut above the discount-store apparel that covered most of the kids in the background. The camera person, a girl, said, "First day after vacay and Grace's outfit is TDF, as usual."

Linc said, "TDF?"

"To die for. Don't you read the slang updates?"

"You're funny."

Onscreen, Grace gave a wicked smile, spoke in a smooth, honeyed-apples drawl as she pointed to various parts of her ensemble. "Nine West, Nicole Miller…"

The girl behind the camera broke in with a sycophantic, "That is so tope."

Grace's face was fine-boned but not especially pretty; plain brown eyes darkened with ire at the interruption. "And the blouse," she continued, "Isaac Mizrahi from Nord's, NOT the discount line, thank you." She struck a model's pose, flipping brunette locks cut in a chiseled style with high-end highlights, and flashed a haughty grin. "Shovel those guts and save your pennies, bitches."

The image cut off. Natasha asked, "Shovel those guts?"

It was Randall who replied, "Entrails disposal, it's where you start when you first get hired at Virginia Meats, unless you know someone. Ten fucking hells is what it is." With a flourish, he double-clicked on the next file.

The next video took place in a bustling school cafeteria, focusing on a frumpy, overweight girl with downcast eyes as she plodded by with her tray. Natasha could hear the same nasty grin in Grace's voice as she murmured, "Those are the same jeans. They *are*."

A deep-voiced new girl said, "No way."

"She wears like, one pair of jeans the whole week."

The brown-noser from the first video chimed in with, "All year!"

Grace replied, "That's why she stinks so bad." A moment later she said, "OMG, those are guy's jeans. She wears guy's jeans!"

Deep-voice said, "She's swaggin," and they burst into giggles as the image flickered off.

Natasha muttered, "Real sweetheart."

Linc replied, "I think the word you're looking for is 'bitch'."

"So we won't have trouble finding people who wanted her dead." She rubbed the back of her neck as Randall brought up the next chapter in the diary of their dead queen bee.

But the next video was very, very different.

The image onscreen twisted this way and that around a trendy teenage bedroom. Through the window was the darkness of night. The voice behind the camera was Grace's, but it took Natasha a moment to recognize it; this time, it was raw and distraught, the breathing quick and shallow.

"What the fuck," said the voice. The image was a blur in places as Grace covered every inch of the room, past high-end electronics, canopy bed, vanity, bookshelf. "What the fuck. What the fuck!"

She's afraid. Natasha sharpened, leaned in.

The next video was much like the first, except this time the phone camera swept around a well-appointed living room. The television was on, snacks and soda on the coffee table. Again, a nearby window showed it was night.

"It's gone." Grace's voice was twisted with fear. "It's gone. Okay. It's gone." The image spun and shuddered as Grace dropped the phone onto the coffee table. "It was so horrible. Oh, God. Oh my God." The video rolled on, the image fixed in a cockeyed view of a ceiling fan, as Grace fought to calm herself.

Natasha dimly heard Linc ask, "What the fuck?"

Randall silently brought up the last video. It was Grace, addressing the camera this time, and Natasha almost gasped at the change in her. This Grace was disheveled, her $200 hairstyle scraggly and unwashed, her face devoid of makeup. Clad in a baggy sweatshirt, she huddled in what had to be her bedroom closet, her face contorted in despair. Tears flowed as she spoke. "I'm not crazy. I'm not crazy. I'm not. I didn't do anything. I didn't do anything. Why, God, why? Why!?" The image froze.

Randall said quietly, "There's one or two more I think I can retrieve, but it will take a while."

Linc replied, "I'll sign off on the overtime."

"You are my hero."

Natasha asked, "What are the dates of those last three videos?

Randall checked. "Bedroom was last Monday. Living room the day after. Closet was… Thursday."

Linc ventured, "Suicide?"

Natasha regarded the screen. "What could scare her so badly that she'd video herself like that?"

"Like what?"

"No makeup? That sweatshirt? A girl like her?"

She stared at the screen, at Grace's terrified, tear-streaked face.

"She wouldn't be caught dead."

Fifty yards into Grace's neighborhood, Natasha knew they were in a very different part of town.

"He gave us the stink-eye," she said, twisting around to eyeball the figure they had just passed. "That old guy. He did!"

Linc was blasé. "Yeah, he probably did."

She turned back around and stewed. "I mean, he wrinkled his *nose*. You've got to be fucking kidding me.

Can't we turn around and cite him for something?"

"Like what?"

"Loitering."

"On his own lawn?" He smiled. Through the window, a line of garish nouveau-riche mansions went by as they drove past. "Not too many people in this town can afford to be snobs, so they stick together. You gotta expand your horizons, Dee-tective Briggs, stop hangin' out in all those trashy neighborhoods, like you did back in the city."

"If you remember, that's where the crimes happened." They lapsed into a peaceful silence. It had taken no time at all for her to feel again the comfort of their banter, and she was already starting to not care what that could mean.

Another mansion loomed ahead, the sole occupant of its cul-de-sac. It was as ugly as it was huge, a hideous jumble of corners and peaks, sided with ridiculous stamped concrete made to look like stone. The car creaked to a stop on a driveway that didn't have a single tire mark or oil stain. Natasha blinked as the midday sun reflected off of it.

As they got out, she said, "So what don't I know about Denise Randolph?"

"She's a bitch."

She pondered the house. "A rich bitch, then."

"Like you said, she's got money and wants everybody to know it. Not even her money, it's her dad's."

"Gerald Randolph, right?"

"Yeah. He's the one who owns everything. They got slaughterhouses, processing plants all over the place. They take the animals the other companies rejected, only hire illegals and white trash 'cause they work for nothing and don't complain. Ever had BigMart baloney? Buck ninety-nine a pound?"

"If I did, I wouldn't admit it."

"Supposedly Denise runs the local plant, but

everyone'll tell you she never goes there. Calls the mayor to get her speeding tickets wiped out. Grace is – was – her only kid. Husband's deceased."

They climbed the porch steps, passing through a grotesque gothic arch built as an extension to the two-story foyer. The front door itself was plain white and surprisingly unadorned. Just as Linc raised his finger to ring the bell, Natasha quipped, "She must pack a lot of meat."

Linc's entire body quivered as he tried to keep himself from busting out laughing. Both their faces twisted and stretched as they clamped a businesslike expression over their mirth. "I shoulda been expecting that."

"Yeah, you shoulda."

The door opened, revealing a severe-looking Hispanic woman, likely in her forties, clad in a crisp domestic's uniform of white blouse and khakis. Her eyebrows were penciled in and her features looked seared into a permanent frown. She asked, "Help you?" with a substantial accent.

Linc said, "We're here to see Denise Randolph."

"Missus Randolph is not here."

Natasha saw Linc frown in surprise, an expression identical to her own. *What the fuck?* "We were supposed to meet her here at this time," Linc said.

The woman replied, "Yes. I know."

"You know about her daughter?"

"Yes. I know." The woman's expression was still rigid, but Natasha noticed her fingers tapping fingertip to thumb tip, one after the other, index finger, middle finger, ring finger, pinky.

"Well, do you know when she'll be here? We need to talk to her as soon as possible."

"I don't know. Maybe later." Index, middle, ring, pinky.

Natasha began to feel her irritation give way to anger.

They're stonewalling. I can't believe it, they're stonewalling us.

Linc wavered, stymied. He shot Natasha an uncertain look, and pulled out his business card, like a car salesman giving up on the first no. The housekeeper's brown eyes twinkled.

Natasha decided it was time to stop playing nice.

She took half a step forward, physically taking control of the space. "We'd like to see Grace's room, if you don't mind." Linc managed to hide most of his surprise, but his eyes narrowed in quiet consternation.

The housekeeper flinched ever so slightly, the silent drumbeat of her fingers halting. Her expression stiffened further into something cold and almost imperious. "Miss Randolph is not here. You need to come back."

Natasha gave her an earnest smile. "She doesn't need to be here if we're just looking around, does she, Maria?"

She noted with carefully concealed joy how the woman's expression clouded with apprehension. "You know my name?"

"Why wouldn't I know your name, Maria?" She twisted the name like a knife thrust deep. "Is there a reason why I shouldn't know your name, Maria?"

"I… don't know."

Natasha waited a few seconds more in silence. "Now. I'd like to see Grace's room."

"I… guess it is okay." Maria stepped aside. Her hands were no longer tapping their fingertip cadence; they were shaking.

Linc slouched near the doorway of Grace Randolph's bedroom. He looked at the objects scattered atop a bookshelf as if afraid to touch them – a cellophane-covered library book about Patrick Henry, a dusty, antiquated iPod, a purple pen with a pom-pom stuck on the end. The bookshelf was white, made of solid wood, in the same style as the dresser and the canopy bed. The walls were painted a faint eggshell blue and were covered with home-made artwork signed with Grace's initials. There were colored pencil drawings of sailboats and horses, watercolor landscapes, even a decent self-portrait. The room smelled faintly of lavender. Linc muttered, "This is gonna get us in trouble."

Natasha, efficiently riffling through Grace's massive dresser, didn't look up as she responded, "If you're going to get pissed at me, you can go ahead."

"Pissed? Why would I be pissed? We're just doing an illegal search."

"State of California versus Oakley, 2004," she replied, snapping a few photos of the bookshelf with her phone. "Permission granted by a recognized gatekeeper is still permission. That and using the help's first name will get you in anywhere." That had been a lesson from the late Detective Billy Fletcher, and she'd learned it well.

Linc, however, replied, "And this ain't California, for Christ's sake. Gerald Randolph's gonna run for governor next year, everybody knows it. Virginia Meats is the only real jobs left in this friggin' county."

Natasha snapped around to face him. "And someone set that little girl on fire while she was still alive, while she was *alive*, and a day later they're still not in town and we're knocking heads with a fucking housekeeper."

Linc took a step back in retreat, but his affronted expression quickly gave way to a resigned smile. "You're still the Pit Bull, huh."

The warmth that spread across her cheeks had nothing to do with the temperature of the room. She smiled in spite of herself. "Didn't think you remembered that."

"You never let me forget." She relaxed, feeling the tension ratchet down. After a moment, he asked, "So, what are you looking in the dresser for, anyway?"

"You'd be surprised what a girl will hide in her dresser." Before he could reply, Linc's smartphone chirped, and everything changed.

She didn't have to see the name on the screen this time; she recognized the way his posture slumped, the way his muscles stiffened. He raised the phone to his ear and said, "Hey, Babe," with his best game face on. His eyes tightened with irritation as he listened. "Okay, well, I really can't talk right now..." The caller was not pleased. Linc's nostrils flared. "Well, I know that, but I'm... Yeah, I know what the fucking counselor said, I was there too, if you remember... Gina, for fuck's sake... Hold on." To Natasha he snapped, "I'll be right back." He stormed out the door and was gone.

She closed the final dresser drawer on an amazing number of expensive t-shirts, and turned to the vanity. It was littered with a hodgepodge of nail polish bottles, a scattering of papers, and some high-end external laptop speakers with no laptop in sight, a detail she made note of. Natasha considered the disarray, looked from the vanity to the disorder on top of the bookshelf, the unmade bed, the sweatpants and canvas slip-ons that lay about the floor.

On her notepad, she wrote: *didn't clean room - more likely murder?* She would have pegged a finespun girl like Grace as the type who would have cleaned up and organized her space if she was going to kill herself. But the truth was she still knew almost nothing about their victim, and it didn't appear she'd be finding anything out until they met with Grace's friends that afternoon. She opened the first of the vanity's two drawers; it contained a jumble of artsy bric-a-brac — sketch pad, colored pencils, gum eraser, a stick of charcoal. The top paper on the sketch pad had the first rough lines of a drawing of a dog. In the second drawer, among makeup, cotton balls, and emery boards, she discovered a number of small pamphlets. Taking a closer look, she discovered that they were religious tracts, and her eyebrows raised at their titles. "Your Sins Shall Find You!" "You Cannot Hide From Hell!" "Jesus Is The ONLY Salvation!" On the back of each was stamped the name of the church – Divine Worship Center of Blessed Jesus the Deliverer. She noted the address and phone number were local. In her notebook, she wrote: *Where did the Randolphs go to church?* It was a cinch they didn't go to a place like that.

On the back of one of the tracts, next to the church's information, was scribbled a name: *Andy*.

Then, out of the corner of her eye, she saw it.

Movement –

A form –

A woman!

Caught by surprise, she spun to meet the danger but felt something slip out from under her foot, sending her tumbling to the floor. In a feral panic she righted herself, crouched in a defensive posture to confront –

Her own reflection in a full-length mirror.

She plunked back down on the floor, her heart hammering, forced herself through Benson's breathing exercise. *In on four, out on eight. In on four, out on eight.*

Jesus Christ, Briggs. Jesus Christ.

Then, something caught her eye and she glanced up. Taped to the bottom of the vanity drawer was a small memory card. She steadied a trembling hand, pulled it from its hiding place, and gazed at it, thoughtful.

She stood. Through the window she noticed Linc, pacing the front lawn, still on the phone. She could not hear him, but the fury evident in his body language told her all she needed to know.

The housekeeper appeared in the doorway, glaring in petty triumph. "Missus Randolph says you have to go."

The memory card, hidden in her closed hand, seemed to tingle against her palm. "Whatever you say, Maria."

Linc drove in angry silence, the radio blaring the local yokel country station, the AC blasting. Natasha shivered and said, "Stop sign."

In reply, he stomped the brake and she felt her body surge against the seat belt. She asked, "You want to talk about it?"

"No. You find anything?"

She answered, "No." If he'd been on his game, he'd have caught her hesitation.

"I'm going to re-canvas that road, see if there's anyone home who wasn't yesterday."

"I can do it."

"I need something to do."

She turned down the radio and the AC. "Tell me."

"You my mother, now?" But almost immediately, she saw the tell-tale slump in his shoulders. "Sorry. That was a shitty thing to say."

"Yeah, it was. So date night didn't go so well."

"Hell, went great until twenty minutes ago. The counselor said we were 'improving our communication process', whatever the fuck that means." His right hand gestured in angry jerks as he steered with this left. "And now it's not even twenty-four hours, not even a damn *day* goes by and she calls and gets shitty with me again. Not even a goddam day."

She noticed the speedometer. "Slow down for that curve."

"Yes, Mom, I see it." But the car still lurched and squeaked as they rounded a corner. "You know, I do what the counselor says. I don't start shit like I used to. I don't..." He stopped himself, slowed his breathing. For a moment, he looked like he might cry. "Sorry. You don't need to hear this."

"I can handle it."

"Yeah, I bet you can." He paused. A view of scrub lots and what might have once been a sawmill flew by outside her window. "Looks like you got here just in time to save me from blowing this case, huh."

She wasn't prepared for that, and all she could think to reply was, "We're a good team."

He quieted, no more at peace than before but more pensive. "Team. Yeah."

The municipal parking lot materialized through the windshield. Linc parked, and the car's engine rattled into sudden, stark silence. Without looking at her, he said, "I'm glad you're here, Nat. I'm glad you came."

She could no longer put off a call to Benson. She made the call in her truck, the engine and AC running, slouched in her seat like a teenager who hadn't studied.

Albert Benson, M.D., Ph. D., said, "Your voice sounds a little anxious."

His voice, with that bland over-sincerity that psychiatrists put on, was even more annoying over the phone than in person. At least when talking long-distance like this, she could roll her eyes all she wanted without having to answer for it. "I'm working a case."

"A case?"

"Linc is the primary."

"I see." She'd met with Benson a few times back in the city, after the incident that had cost her her job and a lot more besides. She could picture him shifting in his chair, scratching his beard, buying time while he thought of something shrinkish to say. "Tell me about the case."

"A teenage girl got set on fire."

"That sounds awful."

"Yeah. Awful."

"How do you feel about it?"

"About what, exactly?" She found herself twirling her hair around a finger.

"About dealing with a case like this."

She rolled her eyes. "I feel like I want to solve it." Benson was, in his way, a tenacious interrogator, and she resented the shit out of being on the other end of it.

Benson came back with, "So, what's it like working with Linc again?"

It was an attack on a different flank, and it took her by surprise. "It's… good."

"Define 'good'."

"It's fine. It's good. How should it be?"

"How do you think it should be?"

She bit back the urge to scream. McGann had approved her being hired only after Benson had signed off on her, and she had to be careful. "I'm not planning on jumping into bed with him this time, if that's what you're asking."

A pause. "Natasha, you're in a very vulnerable place, right now. Do you see what I mean?"

She hoped he could not hear the sulk in her voice. "Yes. I see it. I'm not blind. I'm being careful."

"Being careful about what?"

The ping of a calendar reminder saved her. "I've gotta go. We're interviewing friends of the victim."

"We should talk again on Wednesday. Same time?"

"Wednesday. Sure, got it. Thanks for the refill."

"Try to think about –" but she was already in motion, pressing "end call" and pocketing the phone, sweeping out of the truck all in one fluid motion. She, much like the truck itself, was a machine whose parts worked smoothly only when fulfilling its purpose.

McGann said, "You'll have to do the interview without Meyers. We can't wait any longer."

Natasha opened her mouth to speak, but her protest never made it past the way McGann's eyes narrowed, precluding any dissent. He followed it with, "See me when you're through," and was halfway back to his office before she could draw breath to speak again.

She tried calling Linc and got voice mail again. She texted "GET HERE NOW!" for the third time. Linc's absence didn't seem to surprise McGann, and that made her more uneasy than anything else.

9:13

Natasha pegged Caitlin and Hannah for the two sycophants from Grace's videos. Caitlin was bottle-blonde and brassy, her hair and fashions all discount knockoffs of Grace's. After writing Caitlin's name in her notebook, Natasha added, *the wanna-be*. Under Hannah's name she wrote, *the sidekick*; the girl had more natural beauty than either of the other two, but seemed constantly in search of something to hide behind. Hannah tried to squeeze herself inside an imaginary shadow cast by Caitlin as the girls sat before Natasha in the conference room, concerned mothers on either side.

Natasha began with, "I'm very sorry for your loss, girls," in her best sympathetic-cop voice, more to gauge their reactions than anything else. Caitlin mumbled, "Yeah." Hannah gave a deep nod.

"We're doing everything we can to get to the bottom of this."

Mumble. Nod.

Not too broken up, she noted. *Either of them.*

"So," she continued, "Can you tell me if Grace was behaving differently last week?"

Caitlin replied. "She kind of got all weird."

Weird. It was an interesting choice of words.

"Can you give me some examples of how she was behaving weird?"

"Monday she was just bitchy…" Caitlin's mother shot her an angry look, and she corrected, "Cranky. She said she had bad dreams. Tuesday she was slugging Crankshaft, which she never does." Hannah nodded in agreement.

"Crankshaft?"

"It's an energy drink. She never drinks those, 'cause she says they're bad for your skin or something. She drinks, like, this fancy tea that has a lot of caffeine, and –"

"Okay, so she wasn't sleeping and she was… cranky.

Anything else?"

"Yeah." Caitlin leaned forward to deliver the juicy part. "By Wednesday, she didn't do her makeup. Or her hair, either. She wore these sweats, I think they were the ones she slept in." She scrunched her nose in disgust. "By Thursday she, like, started to smell. She would never do that. Ever." An earnest, confirming nod from Hannah.

"Was she afraid of something? Did she talk about anyone wanting to hurt her, or maybe something wrong at home?"

The wanna-be warmed to her performance, shaking her head with the same kind of theatrical toss she had copied from Grace. "She just got hateful. Bite your head off for no reason. Thursday I asked her what was her deal and she hit me. Bitch hit me." She pointed to a perfectly unharmed spot on her cheekbone. "I could have a scar like, right here. Friday she didn't go to school."

The story was consistent with the decline Natasha had witnessed on Grace's videos, but it wasn't bringing her any closer to finding a suspect. "Can you tell me if Grace was having problems with anyone?"

For a moment, silence. Then Caitlin said, "She had problems with everybody."

Great.

"Anyone in particular? Anyone threaten her?"

"I dunno." Hannah shrugged in agreement. "A lot of people hated on her on Facebook, but that was it."

Hannah suddenly chimed in. "They were afraid of her."

That was interesting. "Afraid. Why?"

Hannah blushed and her gaze reverted to the table. "Um."

Caitlin stepped in. "She said she could get people's parents fired if they worked at the plant, or hire someone to plant dope on them and get them arrested."

Natasha's eyes narrowed. "Say again?"

"She said like her grandad knew the police chief and

he could frame people up for stuff."

A new impression of their victim began to coalesce in Natasha's mind. "Girls," she asked, "Did Grace have any friends, besides the two of you?"

Caitlin: "Not at school."

Hannah: Shake of the head.

Caitlin continued. "It's not like we were, like, her besties. She always went on about these girls she hung out with in Richmond, and having tea at the Jefferson and all this. She wanted to go to this private school in Charlottesville, but her grandad said no. She was really pissed about it." Off another dagger-look from her mother, she amended, "Annoyed about it. She hated everyone at our school."

"She liked you two, right?"

A knowing glance between the two of them. Then Caitlin said, "Our dads are the assistant plant managers, right below her mom."

Hannah piped up: "The ones who actually do the work."

Caitlin added, "She needed someone to have lunch with."

Natasha was quiet for a moment, considering anew all she had learned about Grace Randolph, finding herself no closer to the truth. "Was there anyone else she spent time with in town?"

For a moment, silence. Then Caitlin said, "She got into the dead house party last week, at least she said she did," and immediately replied to her mother's glare with, "Well it's not like *I* got invited."

"The dead house?"

"Yeah, the house where she got.. where she died. Where that guy killed himself." Another nod from Hannah.

Natasha felt her skin begin to tingle. "Tell me more."

"It's like, some people who hang out there

sometimes. It's supposed to be this big deal but it's just a bunch of older kids drinking and stuff. They don't let high school kids come, unless you get invited."

Hannah's voice again appeared out of nowhere. "High school *girls* get invited."

"So, Grace went to the dead house when? This last Saturday?"

Caitlin nodded. "We figured she was gonna brag all about it on Monday, but, you know, Monday she got weird."

McGann said, "Have a seat, Detective." Something about the man's expression made Natasha feel like she was supposed to salute, but she avoided the urge and sat. His office was run-down but in perfect order, like someone had taken the stereotypical chief's office out of an old TV crime show and assigned an obsessive-compulsive to clean it. It lacked the small perks that a boss in even the most hard-up department could obtain if he wanted, like a larger computer monitor, a fancier chair, his own coffeemaker. A fish tank burbled on a small table in the corner. On his desk were small, framed photographs that he kept turned toward himself.

"Your impressions, so far."

She hesitated. "Sir, shouldn't Linc –"

"I didn't ask for his impressions. I asked for yours."

Something's up. But she knew better than to push the issue.

She took a breath, pulled out her notebook, and set to. "The victim was obviously troubled. The way she declined so quickly over the course of a week means she was dealing with something bad. Or something she perceived to be bad."

"Suicide?"

"Possible. Seems like she was isolated socially. The way she let her appearance slide could point to suicide, indicates a state of despair, loss of a sense of control, but those videos – she was scared. Unless she was actually delusional, I think there was someone who was stalking her, could have abducted her and killed her. Someone she met at this 'dead house' party, or maybe the guy who invited her." She flipped through her notes. "Neighbor who called the fire department gave us the name of Justin, gave us a description of his truck. He's a start."

McGann was silent a moment. "I want you to take over as primary."

She felt her eyes widen in shock before she could collect herself. "But, sir, Linc has –"

"Meyers doesn't have your experience with crimes like this."

"But… he knows the town and the people. I haven't even been here a week."

"He was standing outside the Randolphs' house screaming at his wife on the phone. He's not on his game and you know it."

She felt a hollow twisting in her stomach, felt her heartbeat begin to ratchet up. *Don't make me do this, I can't, I can't.*

"Linc's… a good cop, sir." It sounded weak, and she could see McGann reading things in her expression that she didn't wanted him to know. *Damn it. Damn it. Breathe, Briggs. Breathe.*

"Sure he is. He'll be there to help you." He added, "I already told him."

"I see." She suddenly saw one last way to keep from having to bear the weight of this case, and grabbed for it. "If I'm to be the primary, sir, I have to ask, have you thought about bringing in the state police? The extra resources they could give us…"

McGann's voice remained level, but his eyes narrowed into the same pointed glare she had watched him give Linc the day before. "We take care of our own problems, Detective."

She closed her notebook and started thinking of the

pill bottle as she rose. "I'm on it, sir."

He handed her a piece of paper. "I spoke with Denise. She'll meet you at her lawyer's office late this afternoon."

"Her lawyer's office?"

His face was unreadable as he replied, "It's the Randolphs." As she was walking out, he added, "And don't talk to Merriman."

The police building was old; the smells of mildew and new carpeting collided in her nostrils as she exited McGann's office. The walls were painted a dim yellow that seemed halfway to gray in the washed-out fluorescent light. Her desk was in a crowded clump of cubicles in the small bullpen area outside McGann's office. The space between the cubicle cluster and the wall was so narrow she wondered how Linc made it to his desk without having to walk sideways.

One of the bolts in her chair was loose, and it required her to balance precariously; it squeaked in rhythm as she subtly rocked back and forth, tried to collect her thoughts. *I'm the primary. Fuck. Fuck. Fuck.* Benson would be concerned. Linc would be all kinds of pissed.

And me?

She was terrified, and that worried her. She was also thrilled, and that shamed her.

She popped a pill, picked up the phone, and dialed Linc's number.

She was about to leave for the lawyer's office when her office phone rang. "Detective Briggs."

"Detective? It's Eddie Shifflett."

"Eddie. What's up?"

"Well, I just… wanted to apologize for the way I lost it out there. Didn't have the chance to tell you before."

"It's okay. Happens."

"Yeah, well. Thanks. Heard you're the primary,

now."

She stifled a groan. *Justice moves fast in this town.* "Guess I am."

"Well, good luck."

"Thanks. I'll see you around."

She was about to hang the phone up when Eddie blurted, "How's it been going? You got any leads?"

She frowned. "Not much. Got something for me?"

"Me? Oh, no. Just asking. Sorry, we do that 'round here."

"Oh. Okay."

"Well. Thanks." And the line went dead.

She hadn't eaten all day, save for some dry toast to deal with the queasiness from her hangover that morning. It was now after three, and the ache from her hunger was beginning to reach up into her eyes. She pulled into the parking lot of Wright's Crossing's only coffee shop. At least if she was late, her time with Linc before interviewing Denise Randolph would be short.

Five minutes later, she was almost to the door, double-venti in one hand and a bag of industrial croissants in the other, when from behind she heard, "Detective Briggs."

She didn't place the voice until she turned to face the voice. "Merriman." He stood, digital recorder in hand, smooth as a used car salesman.

"Any comment on your battlefield promotion?"

Having to turn to face him had checked the momentum that would have carried her out the door. *Bastard, he's better than I took him for.* "My what?"

"Being made primary investigator. Quite an honor for your first week on the job."

He would have been a major irritation even on a good day, but his recorder was on, and there were people in the shop, mostly shirts and ties having business coffees at this time of day, so she tamped down her response to a terse, "I'm afraid I'm in a hurry, Mr. Merriman." She shouldered the door open, felt the flush of the afternoon heat, and cursed herself for not parking closer to the door.

The reporter's voice, unfazed, spoke up from behind her. "Was Detective Meyers experiencing any problems with the case? Did Chief McGann decide your experience in Richmond P.D. gave you an edge?"

"'Fraid you'll have to ask Chief McGann." She walked with long strides to keep him at a distance. Her coffee sloshed against the inside of the cup.

"If you're on your way to speak to Denise Randolph, you don't have to hurry."

She stopped short, only feet from her truck, faced him again. "Excuse me?" She squinted from the sun behind him.

"Given she was supposed to be making a trip to the main office in Manassas, she should have been back yesterday, but Mrs. Randolph likes to take the long way home, especially when she ditches a company meeting and her daughter for a trip to Belize." He gave her the sly, we-both-know-the-score smile that was supposed to make her feel like talking.

Christ, how well-connected is this guy?
Don't take the bait. Don't.

"Nice talking with you, Merriman." She tucked the croissant bag under her arm, rounded the front of her truck, and opened the door.

But he was there, just outside the truck's door before she could close it. "Look." He pressed the "off" button on the recorder and pocketed it. "The Richmond news crews are already here, you know. Cable news guys should be here tomorrow, seeing as it was a white girl who died. And McGann's going to feed you to them if you don't solve it before they get mean. I can help you, Detective. You need friends, here."

She gunned the engine. "You want to help me,

Merriman, make sure I don't run over your toes."

Merriman pissed her off even more by being right. Denise Randolph wasn't there.

She paced with a feline intensity. "I don't fucking believe this." The pinch-mouthed receptionist looked up and scowled at her choice of words. Natasha flopped back down on an unforgiving wooden chair for the third time, sneezed at the musty law-office smell for the fourth. The clock on the wall indicated it was nearly six.

Linc, for his part, had not moved a muscle, staring at a generic inspirational poster ("Teamwork") in front of him with a face scrubbed of all expression. "It's the Randolphs."

"I keep hearing that."

"You'll keep hearing it more."

She said, as gently as she could, "We need to talk about this."

He shifted his gaze from the poster to his hands. "No, we don't. You're primary, that's all."

"You're pissed. You should be."

"It's McGann's call."

"That's not what we're talking about."

"I'm doing the best I can, okay? It sucks. It's not your fault." His gaze drooped, along with the rest of him. "It's probably better this way. The shit I've got going on right now." The receptionist gave another reproachful look.

Natasha thought of returning the girl's self-righteous scowl with her own patented cop glare, but at that moment a door beyond the waiting area opened and in shuffled the lawyer. Rodney Palmer, attorney at law, was a mousy, comb-over type with an expensive suit that hung from him at odd angles. Natasha rose to speak, but he cut her off with, "I'm afraid Mrs. Randolph has been delayed."

Delayed. She felt her frayed patience reach its limit.

"Delayed." She chewed on the word for a moment, instructed her jaw to unclench long enough to speak. "Sir, Mrs. Randolph is aware that her daughter was burned to death, possibly murdered, almost two days ago?"

Rodent-like eyes blinked, unfazed. "Mrs. Randolph is aware and is doing everything she can to get back here as quickly as possible."

She heard her voice rising, felt Linc's urgent "shut up" vibrations beside her and ignored them. "Sir, just how long does it take to drive from Manassas to Wright's Crossing? She could have taken a Greyhound bus and gotten here by now."

Palmer blinked, implacable. "Mrs. Randolph has been unavoidably delayed. She will speak to you tomorrow morning."

Tomorrow *morning*.

His nose hairs needed trimming; she stifled an urge to yank them out. She relaxed her face and hoped her body would follow. "Well then, I assume she's given permission for us to search her daughter's room?"

"She will most likely allow you to search the room after she has gotten back and spoken with you."

Linc saved the day, breaking in with, "Have Mrs. Randolph call us first thing when she gets back," and deftly steering Natasha toward the exit before she could explode.

She breathed deeply of the stifling outside air, felt the croissants churning in her stomach along with her anger. She heard Linc say, "Let it go."

"She did this on purpose, didn't she?"

"Let it go."

"Fuckers," she muttered as he led her to her truck. "Fuckers." She tasted bile in the back of her throat and thought, in an oddly detached way, that she might cry. She breathed, *in on four, out on eight*, but felt no better.

Linc asked, "So, what's next?"

It took her a moment to realize what he was asking.

She noted how low in the sky the sun was. Denise Randolph had planned this, had told the lawyer to make them wait, to waste the rest of their day. *But why?* "It's late. I'm going to go over everything at home tonight and we'll figure out the next move from there."

He hesitated a moment before asking, "You want me to review it with you?"

Yes. Yes, I do.

"No, I'm good. Maybe you can get started tracking down this Justin guy."

"Got it." He turned and moved toward his car.

"Linc?" He turned back toward her.

"Yeah?"

"Nobody's cried for her. The housekeeper, her friends, nobody. What am I missing?"

Linc's face seemed florid in the waning light. "You're not missing anything. Maybe that's the sad part."

She was halfway home before she realized she hadn't asked him where he'd been all day.

Her living room was another half-assembled space. Unpacked boxes shoved into corners, a couch, a coffee table. A television that was too small for the room displayed a cooking show, but she had turned the sound off.

Natasha perched on the couch, barefoot in t-shirt and sweats, her damp hair pulled back in a haphazard ponytail. The clutter on the coffee table included photos, reports, a legal pad, her laptop. The wine glass in her hand contained white this time, only her second glass; she had promised herself it was the last one of the night. She shifted her feet and felt the coolness of a new patch of floor.

There was a conference call scheduled for tomorrow morning to go over the results of the autopsy, but the distance to the Medical Examiner's office in Richmond had ruined her hopes of observing the autopsy firsthand. On a whim, she'd called McGann and asked if they could request a warrant to search the house without Denise Randolph's permission, which had proven to be a mistake; the man's evil eye could travel right through the phone.

Maybe he's testing me, trying to make the new girl cry.

That thought made her smirk with satisfaction as she inserted Grace's memory card into her laptop.

Onscreen, the security software finished scanning the card. "No threats detected."

If the card turned up anything useful, she'd "find" it when they finally had the chance to make an official search. If not, she'd dump it. She took another sip, savored the dry sweetness of the Riesling, and beheld onscreen a long column of picture files. She clicked open a few at random. They were photographs, snapshots that Grace had taken with her phone and dumped onto this card, no doubt to hide them. There had to be almost a hundred.

She tapped the "slide show" button, and blinked in surprise.

The first set of photos was of a gang of rough-cut young people, most of them in their twenties, it looked like. Harley t-shirts, ball caps, ripped jeans, a few black-toothed grins from the meth addicts in the room. The photos showed them drinking and carousing in the shabby living room of the house where Grace's body had been found. In several photos, the girls among them lifted their shirts and bared their breasts.

Including Grace.

Holy shit.

"Grace, girl," she said aloud, "those don't look like Young Republicans to me." She'd assumed the people at the "dead house party" would be older versions of Grace, and she'd been very wrong. What she had was a whole roomful of prime suspects who couldn't afford good lawyers.

On her notepad she wrote and underlined twice: *Find Justin.*

Out of the corner of her eye, on the periphery of her notice, the clock on her laptop blipped to 9:13.

And everything changed.

The lights dimmed. The laptop screen went dark. The television blinked off.

Natasha looked about in the sudden, cold silence. *What the fuck?*

The laptop came back to life first. Instead of the snapshots, a video appeared, jerky, handheld, a phone camera video taken in a black-dark room. The camera's small light was the only source of illumination, and the image was speckled, pixelated. Even so, it was easy to recognize the subject.

Grace.

The girl's appearance was only slightly more put-together than in the closet video; she wore a chic-cut tank top, and her greasy hair was at least combed. But her face. The terrified misery from the last video had given way to something deeper, defeat rather than desperation. Tears poured down her cheeks. Her eyes were blank with despair.

"I'm sorry," she sobbed. "I'm sorry. I'm sorry. I'm so sorry."

The phone camera's light revealed just enough of what was behind her – the stairs, that shelving. *The basement.*

"Please forgive me," Grace continued through the hitching of her sobs. "Please forgive me. Please."

Natasha set her wine glass down hard, ignored it as it spilled. The footage looped and began again. "I'm sorry. I'm sorry. I'm so sorry…" The volume was loud. The words rang in Natasha's ears. She tapped the laptop's touchpad to stop the playback.

And nothing happened.

The macabre lamentation continued. "Please forgive

me. Please forgive me." The volume seemed to increase. Natasha cursed, pounded the touchpad, then the keyboard. Nothing. The loop began again. "I'm sorry. I'm so sorry…"

Something was wrong. Wrong. She felt a prickly fear work its way up from her stomach, tasted a sour taste in her mouth that had nothing to do with the wine. The volume increased more, more. The girl's wails boomed throughout the room, painful to her ears. "I'M SORRY. I'M SORRY…" Natasha felt herself begin to tremble as the panic she fought daily began to burn under her skin. She closed the laptop. "PLEASE FORGIVE ME. PLEASE FORGIVE ME…" She flipped the laptop over and yanked the battery.

It did not stop.

The television blinked back on, and the video of Grace appeared there as well, forming a booming, out-of-sync duet with the laptop. "I'M SORRY. I'M SO SORRY. PLEASE FORGIVE ME…"

Natasha sprang from the couch but found she could not run, her instincts confused into paralysis by a threat that she could not define. Her heart hammered as the panic closed around her chest. She clamped her hands over her ears, felt Grace's desperate sobs boring their way into her mind. "Stop!"

"I'M SORRY. I'M SO SORRY…"

"Stop!"

"PLEASE FORGIVE ME. PLEASE FORGIVE—"

"STOP!!"

She grabbed the laptop and hurled it into the television screen. The television screen exploded into sparks. She grabbed a nearby lamp and bashed at the laptop, again and again.

The laptop was in pieces before she realized the sounds had stopped.

She huddled on the couch, sweating and shivering all at once. She fumbled open her pill bottle and washed two

9:13

of them down with the rest of the wine.
    Every last drop.

THE THIRD DAY

Linc knew there was trouble as soon as he saw her.

He'd been shooting the bull with two shift officers, sipping harsh coffee and putting off the day another few minutes, when she came storming in, red-eyed and frizz-haired and furious.

Oh, shit.

For a moment, no one said a word, everyone perfectly still like soldiers in a minefield, afraid to be the first to move. Then Natasha pointed an iron finger at him. "Conference room." He could hear the shift officers snicker behind him as he followed her. *This is bad. This is bad.*

It got worse.

He took a ten-second detour to grab his notepad from his desk, in some desperate hope that she wasn't about to go apeshit, but this wasn't the first time he'd seen that look in her eyes.

She was waiting for him, pacing and twitching in that way he remembered well. It was then he noticed the canvas shopping bag, clutched white-knuckled in her hand. He said, "Okay, what?"

Without a word, she dumped the wrecked remains of

a laptop computer onto the table. For a moment, he could only stare. "What the fuck is this?"

She replied in a voice that was almost a scream. "I did not ask to be primary! I did not pull it out from under you!"

"Nat, what –"

"You said, 'It's okay,' 'It's probably for the best.' You just had to do it, didn't you?"

He'd felt a lot of different feelings for her back in the day, and the bolt of pure, high-potency outrage that shot through him now was as familiar as the rest. "Just had to do what? What the fuck are you talking about?"

"Don't, okay? Just don't!" She was close now, chest thrust out, her glowering face inches from his. He could smell the alcohol in her sweat. Wine. "Was it you and Randall? Program that card to go buck wild on my laptop and fuck with my head? Was it?"

"Card. What card, what fucking card?"

"I said don't!"

"And I said I don't know what the fuck you're talking about!"

"The memory card! The one I found under Grace's desk! The one you obviously put there!"

He took a step back; it was that or punch her in the face. "Oh, Jesus. Don't tell me you took something from that room. Don't even tell me."

"My first case, my second fucking *day* here, and you sabotaged me. You're fucking with my case!"

He felt like his head was doing a complete three-sixty around on his neck. His muscles twitched with the urge to break something. "Is this really happening? Am I really hearing this wild bullshit coming out of your mouth your first week on the job?"

"You're the one who brought me here. You're the one who told me to apply!"

"So I'm trying to screw with your case. Me. The guy who went to the mat to get McGann to hire you. Do you even hear yourself? Do you even know what you're saying?"

She didn't reply, but he saw her rage trance finally crack. "Nat," he said, "for fuck's sake, nobody's trying to sabotage you. Because besides me, nobody cares."

She was silent a moment, and then asked, in a voice that was half-challenge and half-pleading, "If I told you something crazy, would you believe me?"

He opened his mouth to say yes, but what came out was, "We just got the call Denise Randolph is back. Maybe you should go interview her. I've got a lead on Justin."

Without another word, she swept the laptop remains back into the bag and stalked out.

He stood there for a moment after she was gone, and belatedly began to feel the real weight of what he'd done by bringing her here.

What do I do?

His phone buzzed in its holster. The screen read, GINA.

Christ, what do I do?

Maria the housekeeper opened the door. Without a word, she turned and led Natasha through the mammoth two-story foyer and into the living room area that she remembered from Grace's video.

Denise Randolph was everything Natasha had expected, a thin, taut-strung woman whose scowl wrinkles had aged her beyond her years, who wore her boutique outfit like a hazmat suit. Her hair was dyed caramel blonde, but Natasha could see traces of Grace in her features. Palmer the attorney sat next to her on the couch. A tea set had been set out on the coffee table, but neither of them offered Natasha anything.

"Mrs. Randolph," Natasha began, extending a hand, "I'm –"

"Please sit down." The voice was rather deep for a woman, the clipped diction no doubt learned at the same school as her posture.

So this is how we're going to play it. Natasha sat. The veneer of calm she'd managed to apply on the way over from the station trembled, but held.

"I've spoken to Chief McGann and I've decided not to press charges over your illegal search of my home," was how the interview began.

Natasha kept her expression calm and professional, but again it took work. "I appreciate your help, ma'am. Naturally we want to do everything we can to –"

"What do you want to know?"

Natasha surprised herself by how close she came to grabbing the silver tea tray and denting it with the woman's head. She opted to cut to the chase. "Tell me about Grace."

Denise was silent a moment. Then, "Grace wasn't the kind of girl this should happen to."

Natasha waited for her to elaborate, but she was silent. *Bitch.* "Did anything about her behavior change recently?"

The woman's eyes narrowed as she replied, "Grace hit a rough patch about a week ago."

"Can you explain?"

"She stopped taking care of herself. She wouldn't sleep." In a tone of utter distaste, Denise added, "She had these… hysterical episodes."

Hysterical episodes. Natasha leaned in. "Please tell me about them."

Denise pressed her lips together into a scowl. "It's… hard to explain. She would be crying, sometimes screaming. She didn't make sense. She seemed to think someone was… stalking her, someone wanted to hurt her. She would say she saw someone in her room or somewhere else, but there was never anyone there. It seemed to be… around the same time every night."

That got Natasha's attention. "What time?"

"I don't know, exactly. Nine o'clock. No, perhaps a little after."

"Did she ever say who this person was or try to describe him?" She had a thought and added, "Maybe drew a picture?"

Denise gave an exasperated sigh. "Grace used the word 'she' once or twice, but I wasn't patient with her about it. I think you're giving too much credence to some teenage drama, Miss Briggs."

Natasha replied, "I go by Detective Briggs when I'm on duty, if you don't mind," and enjoyed watching the woman's anger lines deepen. Denise did not speak. Natasha stayed silent. She thought at random about how sterilely clean this room was. The lawyer refilled his teacup and again no one offered her any.

The silence stretched to the point of discomfort. Denise broke first. "I had her tested for drugs. I made an appointment with a psychologist for this week, but of course…" Natasha saw her ramrod posture slacken just a touch. "I didn't know what to do. Grace was already going through a difficult phase."

"Could you tell me what you mean by 'difficult phase?'"

In an instant, the armor was back. "I don't see how that's relevant. She's a teenager. What more can I tell you?"

Even through the haze of her lack of sleep and the ache in her head from the adrenaline crash after her dustup with Linc, Natasha realized it. *There's something you don't want me to know. About her. Or you.*

She kept her voice even when she said, "Mrs. Randolph, we really need to know all we can about what was going on in Grace's life. Were there people she was hanging out with that – "

"What people? What are you talking about?"

"Her friends said that she had gone to a party at a

place called the 'dead house' last – "

Denise pounced like a haughty tiger. "Just who do you think my daughter was spending time with?"

"I just meant – "

"Where did you hear about this 'dead house'? From those *friends* of hers at school?"

"Mrs. Randolph –"

"That's all you've got, isn't it?" Denise ignored the lawyer's cautionary look. "High school gossip." She rose imperiously. "A goddamned... *rumor* about going to a party where she would never, *ever* go."

Natasha also rose, more incredulous than angry. "Mrs. Randolph, for God's sake, I'm trying to help you."

The woman leaned forward with a smile full of delighted spite. "And it looks like you're doing about as good a job as you did catching that drug dealer in Richmond. Doesn't it?"

The words hit Natasha like a brick. Her cop façade cracked. "What?"

"Maybe trying to ruin good people is how you got things done at your last job, Miss Briggs, but it's not going to get you very far in Colvin County."

Natasha felt something dark and dangerous open up in her, something she had worked hard to keep at rest. She brought herself nose to nose with Denise Randolph and said, in a tone that was all the more dangerous for how calm it sounded, "Mrs. Randolph, we are trying to find the person who murdered your *daughter*."

Denise's icy glower did not waver. "You will not find him here." She turned and headed for the stairs.

Natasha could see the truth, and it spilled from her before Denise had made it up the second step. "You don't care. You don't care if we find him or not."

Her words stopped Denise cold. She turned; her lordly expression cracked.

Natasha closed the gap between them in three strides. "People will tell me to back off because you're grieving, but I know grief. You're not grieving." Her breaths came short and harsh. "Someone set fire to your daughter. While she was still alive. And you, you're worried about people finding out that she went to a party? With a bunch of dirty *rednecks*, is that it?" Ice crystalized in her chest as she saw her words confirmed in Denise's eyes.

The lawyer was suddenly beside her. "This conversation is over."

Natasha did not take her gaze away from Denise's rage-flushed face. "You will allow me to search this house, or I will obtain a search warrant and maybe even charge you with obstruction of justice. I am going to find the person responsible for your daughter's death, Mrs. Randolph, with or without your help."

She was at the front door before Palmer caught up with her. "Any further questions you may have," he said, pressing a card into her hand, "please have Chief McGann call me."

After she discovered herself driving eighty in a forty-five zone, she pulled off the road and called Benson's cell. God was on her side and Benson answered. She raged, he listened.

"It was her daughter," she seethed, hot blood pounding in her ears. "It was her child. She was supposed to take, take care of her. She was supposed, supposed to *protect* her. That was her job. It was her *job*."

Benson, God bless him, kept quiet and let her talk.

Autopsies were discussed via video chat in the conference room. Natasha came in five minutes late, sliding into a seat next to Linc, who didn't look at her as he pulled up the documents on a monitor in front of them. A wide-screen monitor on the wall displayed an image of the medical examiner, a ferret-nosed mince whom Linc addressed as Murray. What little Natasha could see of the office behind Murray was a war zone of clutter, including a crime scene photo of a nude female murder victim tacked to the bulletin board like a pinup.

Murray nibbled constantly from a bowl of candy, slurping his words as he said, "You guys put me off barbecue for a week, Meyers."

"Thought you were on a diet."

"I was, and look what you've done. Had to eat a whole box of donuts to get over it."

"You're breaking my heart and making me hungry."

Natasha felt her jaws clench. "The autopsy?"

Murray looked to Linc, but when Linc remained silent he hurriedly crunched through the candy in his mouth. In the video chat's mediocre sound quality, the crunching sounded like boots on snow. "Cause of death was heat shock, as well as asphyxiation from inhalation of smoke and fumes." He consulted a report. "Full-thickness burns on about… seventy percent of the victim's body. Gasoline was the accelerant."

"Hot and fast," Linc murmured, more to himself than to her or Murray. He had angled himself toward the wall screen, his body language closed off from her, and she found herself not caring.

"Any injuries besides the obvious?"

Murray's right hand seemed to reach for the candy automatically as the other flipped a page in the file. "Nothing to speak of. No gunshot or stab wounds. There could have been some blunt force trauma that would be tough to find under all that charcoal, but the contraction of the muscles indicates she was alive when the fire was lit. Pretty gruesome." It sounded like "grooshumm" as he tried to talk around another piece of candy.

Natasha rubbed at her temples. *We're nowhere. I'm nowhere.* "What else have we got?"

Murray continued through his report, seemed about

to speak, but checked himself. "Well, let's see…" He continued on to the next page. "Stomach contents include tuna salad – had little bits of pickle, you don't see that every day. No alcohol or drugs in the system. Not much else to say."

Something about the rhythm of this consult was off, and she realized what it was. "What about sex?"

Murray blinked, his mouth working silently for a moment before he actually spoke. "Um, what?"

"You didn't mention whether or not she was sexually active or pregnant."

"Oh. Oh, sorry." He made a show of consulting his report. "Yes on sexual activity, no on pregnancy. Anything else?"

She was silent a moment and then replied, "No. I'll email you if I have – if we have any other questions."

Murray signed off without another word. Natasha turned to Linc. "What's with him?"

"Hates to talk about sex. He and his wife have separate beds."

"Sounds like you know him pretty well."

"He's a local guy. McGann got him set up there."

"Is he reliable?"

"Yeah, he's reliable." She was silent as she reviewed the report on the screen before them. After a minute, Linc said, "So."

She kept her eyes on the autopsy photos. "So what?"

"What did Denise Randolph say?"

"Not much." She intra-mailed the autopsy file to her own account. "Where do the Randolphs go to church?"

His voice was apprehensive as he replied, "Saint Mark's Episcopal. It's where all of them go. Why?"

She rose and headed for the door without answering. He asked, "Where are you going?"

"I have a case to solve." And she was gone.

9:13

Natasha wasn't surprised by what she saw when she pulled up to the Divine Worship Center of Blessed Jesus the Deliverer. It was a ramshackle concrete box in desperate need of a paint job, the gutter askew here and there, a rotting windowsill or two. The parking lot was cracked and potholed and long overdue for repainting the lines.

A church for people who thought that God wanted them to be poor. She felt a familiar sinking feeling in her stomach.

The inside was little different than the outside. Dim fluorescent lighting and a mildewy smell greeted her as she entered. The floor was carpeted in a discount-remnant blue and was worn threadbare in places. A hallway turned off to the right, and a door to the left was marked "Office."

Why would a girl like Grace Randolph come here?

In the office she found a receptionist area with a battered metal desk, a few ratty chairs, some apocalyptic "End Times" posters on the walls, but no people. Taped to the desk lamp was a note: "Downstairs in the kitchen." Now she'd have to go deeper into this place.

It was, she thought, proceeding past doors marked with hand-painted Sunday school signs, the feeling you got when you saw someone a hundred yards down the sidewalk coming toward you, someone you never wanted to speak to again, but with each step you came closer, with nowhere to turn off. She knew well the stink of passion and despair that clung to the walls of this place. Momma had dragged her to churches like this one every Sunday for the first nine years of her young life. It was all too familiar and it made her stomach churn, made the breath feel heavy in her lungs. She found the stairs at the end of the hallway as it turned left toward the closed doors of the sanctuary, and descended.

She emerged moments later into a dingy fellowship hall. The only light shone from a room to the left – the kitchen – but enough of it spilled into the hall to help Natasha make out long tables and plastic chairs set in haphazard lines across the room. From the kitchen came the sounds of someone bustling, utensils clanking. The sounds seemed distorted as they echoed about the tiled floor and concrete walls. Her footsteps squeaked on the floor as inhaled the heady odor of tuna fish in the stale air.

The kitchen had a single occupant, a young woman who couldn't be more than twenty or so. She was of average build, dressed in the standard church mouse uniform – button-down blouse, denim skirt that went past the knees, and scuffed flip-flops. The feet in those flip-flops were dirty and the toes weren't painted. Her brunette hair was luxuriant but devoid of any style, bundled back into a careless braid. Her movements were quick and skittish as she looked up from an industrial-size can of tuna. Nearby were an equally large jar of mayonnaise, a mixing bowl, loaves of sandwich bread. The young woman applied a smile to a face that didn't look like it smiled often. "Help you, ma'am?"

"I'm looking for Reverend Pyle."

The young woman's voice was quiet, but rough-edged. "Oh, you mean Bishop Pyle, ma'am."

Bishop. You've got to be kidding me. "Bishop Pyle, then."

"I'm sorry, he's doing his hospital ministry right now." She fidgeted under Natasha's gaze; her hands twitched as if they sought escape. "Something I could help you with?"

Natasha nodded toward the sandwich fixings. "Having a party?"

"We're doing the lunches at the soup kitchen this week."

"Oh."

The woman went back to work. She dumped the contents of the tuna can into the bowl, followed by a glob of mayo, stirred the mixture with a large wooden spoon. Natasha continued, "Can you tell me if there's someone named Andy who goes to this church?"

The woman flinched, then recovered and applied the smile again. "That'd be me, ma'am. Andy Wagner." After a moment, she added, "My daddy wanted a boy."

Natasha showed her badge. "I'm Detective Briggs. I need to ask you some questions, if you don't mind."

"Oh." Andy kept her attention focused on her work. The stink of the tuna was overpowering in the small room. "Be glad to help if I can."

"You've heard what happened to Grace Randolph?"

"Yes, ma'am. God rest her soul."

"So you knew her."

For a moment, Andy looked stricken. "Oh. No, no," she stuttered, "I mean, not like we were friends or anything."

"She wrote your name down on one of the church flyers."

Andy added another can of tuna, another glob of mayo. Her hands trembled ever so slightly as she worked. "Well, I wouldn't know about that, ma'am. I mean, she was only here once, at the Wednesday night service."

"It's funny, I thought her family went to Saint Mark's."

"I wouldn't know about that, ma'am."

Bullshit.

She only replied, "I see," and let the silence linger for a moment. More tuna. More mayo. The bowl was near full and the ugly pink glop inside would spill over if any more was added. "Can you tell me what she was like that night? Did she seem... happy? Sad? Nervous?"

"I wouldn't really know, ma'am. She was... kind of quiet, kept to the back, you know."

"Did you sit with her? Talk to her?"

"No, I... sit toward the front, usually."

Of course you do.

Natasha watched as Andy reached into a nearby cupboard and pulled out a small container. A jar of pickle relish. With a practiced air, she popped off the lid and dumped the contents into the bowl.

"Little bits of pickle," Natasha said. "You don't see that every day."

Andy relaxed slightly. "My granny taught me that way," she replied with a smile. "The folks always know when our church is making the…" Her smile faded as Natasha lifted an eyebrow.

"Andy," Natasha said, "I think you would know about Grace after all, wouldn't you?"

Natasha watched Andy as she sat rigid at the table nearest the kitchen. Her hands were still; she seemed to contemplate them intensely. "Grace came to the service, like I said. They asked me to sit with her."

"Why?"

"It's… just something we do, try to make new people more comfortable."

"What was she like that night?"

"She was kind of a mess, ma'am. She had bags under her eyes like she wasn't sleeping. Most of the service, she just kind of sat there. Sometimes she'd cry. Then she asked Bishop Pyle would he talk to her."

"Did he?"

"Yes, ma'am."

"Do you know what they talked about?"

Andy hesitated. Natasha lifted the eyebrow again. "Yes, ma'am, I do." She paused again, looked up as if she expected Natasha to say something, quickly shifting her gaze back to her hands. "She wanted him to perform a casting-out."

What the fuck?

"You mean an exorcism?"

"Yes, ma'am. Bishop Pyle… He's got the gift of casting out demons. He rescued a hundred souls all at once one time when he was a missionary."

Natasha watched Andy's hands. They remained still.

"All right. She wanted a…casting-out. Did he give her one?"

"No, ma'am. Not the first time she asked, I mean."

"Why not?"

"Kids like her, I mean, from her side of town, they tricked him once, video'd him and then put it online and made fun of him. So he said no. But Saturday morning, I guess she called him and asked him again, because he asked me to pray with her that day, make sure she was serious."

"Bishop Pyle puts a lot of faith in you."

For a moment, she thought Andy would blush. "I've been going to this church my whole life, ma'am."

"So, you met with her on Saturday."

"Yes, ma'am, she helped me make the sandwiches. We ate some, had some fellowship. We talked at this very table."

"What did she tell you?"

"She said she was being attacked by a demon."

Natasha remained silent.

"She said it was happening every night, these horrible… visions, like having nightmares when you're still awake. She said the demon was… hurting her. Burning her."

Nightmares when you're still awake. A shadow of unease came over Natasha, for reasons that she could not see but could instead only feel.

"How long did she say these 'attacks' had been going on?"

"Close to a week. She said they started the Sunday before. They were getting worse every night."

"Did she have any injuries you could see? Bruises? Scratches?"

"No, ma'am. Not that I could see."

"Did she describe this… demon?"

Andy replied, "No, ma'am," just a touch too quickly, but Natasha decided to let it pass.

"Do you think she'd been doing drugs?"

"I wouldn't know about that, ma'am."

"Did she do or say anything that would have led you to think she wanted to hurt herself?"

Andy replied abruptly, "I decided she wasn't serious."

Up went Natasha's eyebrow again. "That's not what I asked."

Andy looked up from her hands, her gaze suddenly cold and impenetrable. "I could tell, ma'am. She was trying to make a fool of me and I didn't appreciate it."

"Make a fool of you? You in particular?"

Andy's dull brown eyes momentarily flashed with wrath. "Me. Us. The church. I threw her out after that."

It was almost too much for Natasha to take in at once, her victim being stalked by the devil, haunted by an angry spirit. She studied Andy Wagner, looking for some uncertainty in her pale, plain face, silently taking her measure. But Andy remained resolute.

Fuck it. Wrap this up.

She broke the pinched silence with, "Did Grace tell you anything about where she was going? If she was going to see anyone else?"

"No, ma'am. She just left."

"Did she say anything after you told her to leave?"

"She said, 'I'm sorry'."

It was then, looking at Andy's face, that Natasha felt a surge of recognition. "You," she said, "you were at the crime scene. Across the road."

Andy didn't waver. "I was driving by, ma'am. I help out one of our people lives down that way. She lives alone." After a moment, she said, "Not to be rude, ma'am, but they're gonna need those sandwiches soon."

Natasha closed her notebook. "Don't let me stop you."

Andy rose from her seat. Natasha let her get halfway back to the kitchen. "One more thing."

Andy froze, then turned around with deliberate care.

"You could have come forward about this yourself, but you didn't. Then you lied to me about knowing Grace. Why?"

Andy replied matter-of-factly, "I don't like cops, ma'am." Then she turned and scuffed back into the kitchen, her flip-flops popping against her heels as she went.

As Natasha ascended the stairs to leave, the thought struck her.

Is that who I'd be if Momma had lived?

Natasha got a text from Linc as she was booting up her new laptop. "Justin says wasn't there – named 3 who can confirm. Follow up?"

She replied, "Yes," and was relieved to know he'd be occupied for a while.

She had "found" the memory card during the finally-authorized search of Grace's room, a room she could tell had been gone over with a fine-toothed comb in the time since they had been there last. She could feel her heartbeat ratchet up in trepidation as the card clicked into place. She thought briefly of handing it over to Randall to review.

Fuck it. This is mine.

If the same thing happened this time, she'd be prepared, but for reasons she couldn't explain, she knew it wouldn't. The virus scan came up clean. She realized she was holding her breath.

Nothing happened, no horrible, looping video, just the near-endless list of picture files. She put aside what that might mean for her and clicked "slide show."

The photos, except for the fact that Grace was in them, were a mundane collection of party pics. Along with the bare-breast shots she'd seen before, there were the other usual suspects – simulated rough sex against the wall, girls tongue-kissing, young men giving the camera the finger.

But then another series of photos appeared, and these were definitely not mundane.

It only took her a moment to recognize the loud blue color on the walls. It was the upstairs room, the teenage girl's bedroom. And posing naked on the filthy mattress was Grace.

Holy shit.

There were about twenty pictures in all; the girl was not shy.

Grace, what the hell did you get yourself into?

The answer shocked her even more than the photos, as a picture near the end caught the photographer's reflection off the cracked vanity mirror, the face instantly recognizable.

Eddie.

Andy perched on the edge of her bed and could not find peace.

The tiny apartment that surrounded her was a study in sparse and dull. She hadn't set out to make it that way, but after she had assembled the sad array of cast-off furniture among the patchwork of paint and carpet remnants with which the landlord had covered the walls and floor, she'd decided that it was right for the likes of her. God's will.

In her mind, she twisted and probed the memory of her conversation with the detective. The woman had the look, the shadow in her eyes that told of the evil she'd seen. She could still feel that gaze, prickly on her skin.
But her thoughts swelled with animosity as she remembered the stricken face of that rich girl, caught out in her deceit. *No human being can tame the tongue*, the Bible said. *It is a restless evil, full of deadly poison.* Andy had done her own casting-out, had sent the bitch running back to her big house and her wickedness. She had done right. She was sure of it.

9:13

And then, two days ago, she'd been driving back from checking in on Edna Crowther, and stopped when she'd seen the crowd.

Why that house? Heavenly Father, why did it have to be that house?

The question would consume her if she allowed it to. Bishop Pyle would call it the blessing of a test of faith, but Andy knew she was unworthy of such a test. What plan could the Heavenly Father have to place her on that road, the very day Grace Randolph's body was found at that house?

A battered pasteboard jewelry box graced the top of a nearly-barren bookcase. She opened the bottom drawer of the box and pulled out its only contents, an old cell phone. She plugged it into a nearby wall, waited for the ring-ting chime that announced she could use it. No signal bars showed on the tiny screen. She hadn't used the phone in years, for after a certain day almost two years ago, there had no longer been anyone to call.

She kept it, though, even after Bishop Pyle gave her another for the occasional call about church business. With the ease born of many repetitions, she thumbed open the phone's menu, pulled up the voice mail, and pressed OK to play the lone, archived message.

That voice from years ago once again pleaded, *"Andy, Andy please — "*

The message ended in a loud bang-crackle that, after many listenings, she had told herself was static. She played the message again, and then again. After a time, she blinked and realized she was still holding the phone and an unknown amount of time had passed.

She had sinned. She did not understand the nature of it, but she had sinned, sure enough, and God would not show her the way back from it.

It was time to make an offering.

She rose and walked solemnly to the closet. The door creaked open to reveal a tiny, coffin-like space, empty except for two things: a large cross she had nailed to the wall, and a length of logging chain laid on the floor.

She felt her heart quicken in anticipation and dread as she entered the closet and shut the door.

There was just enough space for her to kneel before the cross. The closet floor was uncarpeted, the subfloor exposed; its surface was rough and unforgiving against her knees. She removed her blouse, then her bra, folded and laid them carefully behind her. If there had been any light in that closet, it would have shone on an angry, purple mass of bruises across her back.

She picked up the chain reverently. Then she whipped it over her shoulder with all her might.
She gasped at the brilliant shock of pain, each subsequent blow punctuated by a growing crescendo of cries.

Blows that wound cleanse away evil, said the passage from Proverbs. *Strokes make clean the innermost parts.*

When she was finished, when every nerve in her back sang with agony, she collapsed to the floor and felt God's warmth and love again. For a time, at least, she would again feel clean.

Natasha struggled to stay alert.

Eddie's home was a ramshackle singlewide trailer at the end of an unmarked gravel drive. She'd found no cars in the driveway. Her knock at the front door had gone unanswered. She'd gone back to her truck and settled in to wait.

And wait.

The day's heat lingered even as the sun had dipped below the horizon. She'd rolled down the truck's windows and shed her jacket, but her skin still prickled. Her head buzzed; the trauma of the night and day that had gone by were catching up with her. She winced as she sipped the final lukewarm drops of her coffee. She absently brushed gritty granola bar crumbs off her clothing.

9:13

Her smartphone buzzed again. It was another out-of-state number she didn't recognize. The national press had finally picked up on the story, and someone in the department (Dudley, she suspected) had given out her number. The call was followed by a voice mail, then a text from the same number, all of which she ignored.

She played music on her smartphone to help her stay awake. The screen clock read 9:10.

You should have called Linc, gotten some backup.

The clock read 9:11.

Fuck them. This is mine.

She rested her head against the door panel. The clock blipped to 9:13.

She heard a soft, electric *click*.

The doors had locked on their own.

The phone winked off, dead and silent.

"What the fu—"

The windows began to close by themselves, slowly rising without the whir of the electric motors. She pressed the button to open them; she pressed it again. They continued to slide upward. "Goddamn it. Goddamn it!" The windows snugged into their slots with a glassy kiss and she was sealed in.

She used hostility to deal with the knot of panic that bloomed inside of her. She popped the lock on her door, yanked the handle, and shoved.

It would not budge.

"Piece of shit!" She yanked the handle again, shoved against the door with her shoulder, felt a throb of pain down her arm. She shoved again. Again.

The door would not open.

She could perceive a shift in the air around her, a shadowy, electric chill. She could hear her heart hammering in her ears. She twisted to the right, tried the passenger door, bracing herself against the driver door, shoving with all her might.

Nothing.

She could feel it again, the horrific sensation of something, some outside presence, worming its way into hers, looking into her soul, displeased with what it found.

"Briggs," she gasped. The soggy heat in the car seemed to press on her chest as she tried to breathe. "Briggs, for fuck's sake. For fuck's sake." She pulled out her pistol and aimed for the passenger window. But before she could shoot, something liquid, something dark and viscous, began to pour over the windows, and in moments had blotted out her view to the outside. A trace of moonlight still shone through the liquid obstruction, and the light was red, deep red almost to blackness.

Blood. Blood!

It cascaded down the windows, a river of death come to claim her.

And when a human hand swiped aside a narrow cleft in the blood covering the front windshield, for a moment she had hope. *It's Eddie, it's Linc, he'll save me. He'll –*

She screamed.

The girl. The girl!

Somehow, even in the pitchy night, Natasha could see her, an emaciated, filthy wraith, her clothing in tatters, the heavy chain around her neck. The same girl from the night before.

The awful specter gazed into Natasha's terrified eyes with an expression of pure, wrought-iron malice.

Its voice was a hoarse, meatgrinder growl; she felt it flay at her mind as the thing said, *"Are you sorry?"*

And in an instant, it was gone. Natasha crashed back into awareness, blinded by a sudden white light.

Headlights.

Her truck was unlocked. The windows were down. And Eddie was home.

Her mind reeled, her breath came in gasps, she felt a sheen of sour sweat over her face. But her cop training ran deep, and her body performed the tasks of grabbing her flashlight, exiting the car, as her mind scrambled to catch up. She glanced at her truck. There was not a drop of blood to be seen.

The headlights turned off, revealing a full-size, newer-model pickup. Even in only the moonlight, it was clear that Eddie was one of those guys who took better care of his truck than he did his house. The truck was a diesel, and when the rumble of the engine died, the stark quiet that ensued was unnerving.

Natasha's movement activated a security light on the trailer's porch. It cast half of Eddie's face into a macabre shadow as he exited the truck, stood beside it, looked at her as if he was not sure she was really there.

Natasha said, "Eddie."

Eddie held his arms military-straight at his sides. He murmured, "Detective. I...didn't know you were here."

"Been waiting for you."

"Oh." He looked about to say something more, but stopped, half-gaping at her like a frog.

"You look kind of shook up, Eddie."

"Just...wasn't expecting you, I guess."

"I need to talk to you, Eddie."

Even in the stark yellow light, she could see his face pale. "Well, I don't know."

She slid her hand down to rest on her holstered gun. "I need to talk to you now."

Eddie bolted. She'd been half-expecting it, but he was faster than she was ready for. "Stop! Stop right now!" Eddie raced like a rabbit for the woods beyond his house, while she brought her flashlight and her Glock to bear and sprinted after him.

Her light cut a bright but thin swath through the gloom. She followed the sounds ahead, the rustling of branches and leaves, but the terrain was treacherous, the near-total darkness oppressive. She cursed as she stumbled. Unseen branches scratched her hands and face as she plowed onward. Her shirt was soaked with sweat and she shivered.

She felt feather-light tendrils suddenly caress her face and nearly screamed in panic before she realized she'd blundered into a spider's web. The unbroken web meant he hadn't come this way.

Fuck, he could be anywhere.
Fuck!

She emerged into a clearing and hesitated, trying to re-orient herself in the moonlight. She strained to listen past the freight-train sound in her ears from her heightened blood pressure. Insects chirped in the eerie quiet.

The crack of a broken twig sounded somewhere nearby. She aimed her flashlight and her gun in unison, clicked off the Glock's safety as she swept back and forth, searching. The scents of earth, of sap, of plant life and dead leaves, all were rich in her nostrils, adding to her sense of isolation, exposure. "Eddie Shifflett, come out with your hands up!"

Behind me –

She whirled with her Glock, but once again he was damned fast. A whisper of movement in her ear. Her wrist barked with pain as a large tree branch knocked the gun from her hand, but the momentum of the swing put Eddie off balance. She swung with her elbow; it caught Eddie in his cheekbone but did little to slow his fist. There was a blast of pain in her temple and she felt her legs give out from under her.

In a flash he was atop her, his hands on her throat. His eyes were feral with fear as he throttled her. "I'm sorry!" he yelled. "I'm sorry! I can't let you tell! I can't let you tell!"

Her body forced itself to act as the panic of suffocation hit. She gave his groin a savage jab with her knee, heard him gasp, felt his grasp weaken. She hammered a fist into his face, swung an elbow-chop to the throat. He gave a choked gurgle of pain, scrambled off of her, gasping, trying to crawl off into the safety of the woods.

But Natasha was on her feet, and the branch was in her hand.

In an almost bestial fury, she bashed him with it, over and over again.

She screamed, "You like to hurt women, don't you!" as Eddie cowered against the blows and bawled like a child. "Don't you! Motherfucker! Motherfucker!"

Natasha slumped in a flimsy plastic chair near Eddie's front door. She was dimly aware of others trooping in and out as the search of the trailer continued, but the pain shimmering from the side of her head was all she had the energy to focus on. She said to Linc, "You look like hell."

Linc's face did seem dragged out and haggard as he applied a cold pack to the bruise on the side of her head. "Hell yeah, I look bad. My partner's running around in the woods without backup and getting her ass kicked." She winced at the chill that bit into her temple. "You should've called me."

She took the cold pack and held it in place herself, hoping the bite of the cold would keep her a step ahead of her exhaustion. "I thought this guy was Howdy Doody."

"Yeah, Howdy Doody the brown belt." He wanted to be mad at her, she could tell, but his rebuke sagged into a smile. "Same old Nat. Jump and the net will appear. I'll take you to the ER."

"I don't need the ER."

"Nat, for Christ's sake."

"Just give me a minute, okay, Mom?"

He relented. She closed her eyes and drifted between the chill of the ice pack and the throbbing of her temple.

You should have called him. The voice in her mind was bitter with reproach. *You should have called someone. After what happened to you, not even a year ago, what happened to Billy.*

What the fuck were you thinking?

She took a deep breath. *In on four, out on eight.* There was nothing to do about it now. She felt her mind drift back to equilibrium.

"So," she said, her voice and her thoughts softer. "I'm getting my ass kicked and here you are, handing me the ice pack."

"Yeah."

"Like old times."

"You know, when other people talk about old times, they talk about the trip to Disney World or something."

"You never took me to Disney World."

"You wouldn't take the vacation time."

She could not say what she really wanted to say, so she opted for the next best. "I'm sorry I ripped you up like that this morning."

"It's okay."

"It's not."

She felt his hand close on hers. She opened her eyes and found herself staring into his. They were a strong blue, and their depth was not something you realized at first glance. "Things are gonna be okay, Nat. You're gonna close this case, you're gonna get situated and things... they'll go back to normal for you."

Normal.

The word brought her quickly to a sense of bitterness that just as quickly faltered into sadness. Linc looked surprised as her expression clouded. "What is it?"

She stood and managed not to totter. "What do you think is normal for me, Linc?"

He shrunk a bit, classic man-in-the-headlights. "I...don't know."

She walked back to her car without looking back.

Neither do I.

THE FOURTH DAY

McGann said, "You look like hell."

Natasha rubbed her bleary eyes. "Doctor said don't sleep after a blow to the head." At least he would have said it if she had actually gone to the ER. She now regretted not going, but only because it would have helped her score something better than Tylenol. Her temple had settled down to a dull ache, but only if she moved slowly. McGann let it pass. Before them, a monitor displayed live video of the interview room where a haggard and bruised Eddie Shifflett, dressed in jail orange, sat jittering at the table, one hand cuffed to a ring attached to the wall. "He's agreed to answer questions."

"Didn't ask for a lawyer?"

"No. Waived his Mirandas."

"Does he think he's clever or something?"

A derisive snort. "Not Eddie."

She gathered the manila folder she'd brought with her. "Linc ready?"

"I sent him to review the contents of Eddie's laptop with Randall."

She hesitated. "You want me to interview him alone?"

He nodded toward the screen, his expression inscrutable. "Meyers won't ask the hard questions. I'll be observing."

Shit.

She hesitated again. "Eddie's a department employee. Don't the state boys want in?"

It was a mistake to ask and she knew it. McGann replied, "We take care of our own problems, Detective."

She paused a moment too long before nodding and turning toward the door. From behind her, he said, "All you have to do is pound on him a little and make the official arrest. You can do that, right?"

She hid the surge of equal parts irritation and shame inside her, and replied, "Of course I can," as she left his office.

She walked as slowly as she could without looking like she was dogging. *In on four, out on eight, in on four, out on eight.* There was so much she needed to work out. The horrors of the past three nights, the specter of the terrible young woman. *In on four, out on eight. You've got this, Briggs, you've got this.*

She thought wistfully about the pill bottle as she reached the door to the interview room.

There were different kinds of suspects, and Eddie's classification in her system was "rabbit." He'd bolted when she'd confronted him. Now trapped, he looked up at her with the eyes of a prey animal, electric with uncertainty and fear.

"Eddie."

His eyes tried to avoid the bruises on her neck, but she had loosened her collar to make them more noticeable. "Um," he stuttered, "Linc gonna be here?"

"No."

"Can I smoke?"

"No."

"Can you uncuff me?"

"No."

She opened the file folder and slowly laid out two photographs, one from Grace's naked photo shoot, the other one a shot of her burnt corpse. Eddie flinched and looked away, but said nothing.

Natasha sat down across from him, nonchalant. "Hard to believe it's the same girl, huh?"

Eddie's terrified gaze locked with hers. "There's nothing I can tell you."

"What really impresses me," she continued, as if she was holding a conversation about the weather or sports scores, "is how you managed to hold it together at the crime scene, I mean, up 'til the moment you puked." She felt it, the warm adrenaline beginning to flow, her nerves calming as the cop in her took over.

Eddie replied, "I don't know anything." The cuffed hand twitched.

"Did you plan to kill her? Or was it more like a spur of the moment thing?"

His nostrils flared. *Interesting.* "I didn't do it."

"Eddie." She leaned forward, still cool as a cucumber. When dealing with the rabbit, keeping your cool usually freaked them out worse than being harsh with them. "When I worked in Richmond, there were all kinds of people who knew how to burn someone up without taking the rest of the house. Here, not so many. You're a crime scene tech and a volunteer firefighter –"

"That's just how gasoline burns. You know that."

"And the fact you just happened to call and ask questions about how the case was going?"

"We do that. We do that here. I just…wanted to know."

"Did she break up with you? Sleep around on you? Threaten to tell McGann? Me, I'd be afraid if she told that mother of hers. You'd –"

"LISTEN TO ME!" He shoved the photos and her

folder off the table with his free hand. "Listen!" His scream was raw and desperate. "Listen!"

Natasha sat unflinching, unperturbed. She let several seconds tick by in silence. "Feel better now?"

Eddie broke. He sagged, bowed his head. "I fucked her."

Bingo.

"I fucked her. Jesus Christ, I admit that. Okay. I did that."

"Wouldn't have thought you were her type."

He snorted something like a laugh. "Some rich girls like to work the soup kitchen, some like to fuck rednecks. Drove her mom batshit. Ain't like I was the first."

"There's no calls between the two of you on her phone."

He snorted again. "I ain't that stupid. I gave her a prepaid phone."

"When did you start seeing her?"

He replied by asking, "Can you please uncuff me?" After a moment, he added, "I ain't gonna do nothing. I'm fucked as it is."

She relented and reached across the table to unlock the cuff. As he rubbed his wrist, she asked again, "When did you start seeing her?"

"Six months ago, I guess. She and her class came on a tour of the station. She was asking me all these questions 'cause of what they show on TV. We…got to talking."

"I'd say you did. So what went wrong?"

He looked down at his hands and seemed surprised to see that he was still rubbing his wrist. "I don't know. A few weeks ago, she gets quiet on me, stops texting, won't return mine. I figured she was done with me, you know. Then she sends a text and asks can I take her to the dead house party. So I did. That night, seemed like everything was good again."

She raised an eyebrow. "I'd say it did. So what happened after that?"

"She got quiet again. I figured she was done, you know. Just used me to get into the dead house party."

"Must have made you really mad, getting thrown out with the trash by a girl who's never even had to wash her own car."

Eddie hadn't seemed to hear. "Day before she died I got a text, it just said, 'I'm sorry'."

I'm sorry.

She felt her body stiffen in apprehension. The pain in her temple flared. She should have let him keep talking, but instead she asked, "What do you think she meant by that?"

"How the hell should I know? Maybe she thought she hurt my feelings."

"So what happened the night she was killed?"

"What do you mean, what happened?"

"Two sides to every story. Now's your chance to tell your side."

He looked at her. His lip curled. "What happened was I sat in my damn living room and got drunk alone. Like I always do. That's what happened." He held his head in his hands and began to cry. "I fucked her. Send me to jail, do whatever. But I didn't kill her. I swear, I didn't kill her."

She watched Eddie as he shivered out his tears, and suddenly her certainty of his guilt faltered.

What if he's telling the truth?

She'd been a careful observer of people her whole life, and it wasn't just her cop instincts that warned her now. Something was missing from this picture, something important. It mocked her, maddeningly out of reach through the fog of the pain and the trauma she'd endured. Her instincts told her what she should do. Let Eddie sit in jail for the assault and for corrupting a minor. Keep investigating. Hold off on the murder arrest.

But all it took was one glance at the video camera watching from above to convince her otherwise.

She nodded to the camera, the signal to McGann, and a second later a uniformed officer, Paxton as it happened, entered the room to get Eddie on his feet. Natasha heard herself recite, "Edward Wayne Shifflett, you are under arrest for the murder of Grace Randolph," as Paxton re-cuffed Eddie's hands behind him. "You have the right to remain silent. If you give up the right to remain silent…"

Eddie did remain silent as she finished reading him his rights, the only sound beyond her voice the snicking of the cuffs as Paxton fastened them around his wrists. As Paxton guided him out of the room, Eddie looked at Natasha and said, "I'm sorry I jumped on you like that."

She could not meet his gaze as Paxton led him away.

Andy heard the news from Edna Crowther.

Edna was sixty-seven and morbidly obese, and regularly got skin ulcers on her legs. She was ignored by her family, a pack of Godless trash according to Bishop Pyle, and he had made it Andy's job to minister to her. Kneeling before her enormous charge while the always-on TV muttered in the background, Andy had just begun the ugly work of cleaning, disinfecting, and re-bandaging, all the while struggling against the urge to vomit, when Edna surprised her by speaking. "They caught him, you hear?"

"No, ma'am, who did they catch?"

"Man who burned up that poor girl."

"Oh." The big sore on the back of Edna's right leg had begun to ooze. Andy's stomach went into somersaults. "Who was it?"

"He's a Shifflett, no surprise. He was a policeman or something, can you believe?"

"Oh, mercy."

Edna, in a rare moment of intensity, leaned forward. "Heard he was havin' her, you know? Girl was sixteen and he was havin' her and then he killed her. I swear, by Jesus, I swear."

"Well, I'm sure glad they caught him, ma'am." But Edna had already sunk back into herself and become lost in some TV show about selling houses in Hawaii. Andy finished her chore in silence, saying a guilty prayer of thanks to the good Lord that she had made it through another visit.

She told herself she should be relieved at the news. Grace Randolph was obviously a troubled soul, a girl who had given her body in sin and by coincidence, pure coincidence, was murdered in that house.

As she left, she said, "God be with you, ma'am."

Edna replied, "Ain't been with me so far."

Natasha picked up a call she thought was from dispatch. "Detective Briggs."

"Congratulations, Detective. Quick statement about the arrest?"

She stifled a groan. "How did you get someone to transfer you back here, Merriman?"

"Pays to have friends in low places. Now how about it? Give a local boy a break?"

"You're about as local as I am."

"Hey, if it takes twenty years for them to call you a local like I hear it does, I'm still two years closer than you."

"We'll be holding a press conference this afternoon. Now –"

"Care to answer a few questions for my upcoming profile? 'Young Gun Detective Nails Her First Case?' 'Small-town Girl Makes Good', and all that?"

She bristled. The bruise on her temple throbbed. "Why would you call me a small-town girl?"

An awkward pause. "I...saw where you went to high school. On your Biz-Link profile."

Chagrined, all she could manage at first was, "Oh." She made a mental note to take down the Biz-Link profile immediately.

"You know," Merriman continued, "it's nice to see at least one case from that house get solved."

That caught her interest. "The other one was a suicide. Case closed."

Merriman's tone was a verbal shrug. "So they say."

She shook her head. "Only person more suspicious than a cop is a reporter."

"Have a drink with me?"

"Excuse me?"

"A drink. You know. At a bar and all."

"McGann would kill me, right after he killed you."

"So wear a disguise or something. Do I have to think of everything?"

She half-smiled. "Nice talking to you, Merriman."

"Can I quote you on that?"

She hung up. She could at least respect a guy like Merriman, ambitious, relentless, stuck working the sticks and likely pissed about it. He probably thought that they were birds of a feather; maybe he was actually even attracted to her.

He doesn't know me, she thought, as her smile faded to gloom. *He doesn't know me.*

A while later, she called Randall because Linc wasn't answering his phone. Randall said, "Congratulations on the arrest."

"Thanks. Just curious what you and Linc found on Eddie's laptop."

A confused silence. "Me and Linc?"

"Well, yeah. McGann said the two of you were going through it."

"I've been working on the laptop, but I haven't seen Linc all day."

Linc stewed.

9:13

He had parked in a secluded patch of woods off Langhorne Road, a spot McGann had once pointed out where officers back in the day would bring the pretty female suspects who were willing to work off a charge. He had the motor running and the AC cranked and didn't care about the gas he was using because it was a department car and he was in that kind of mood. Another text from Nat: "Where the hell are you?" followed by one from Gina: "Call me PLEASE."

He couldn't stay here. McGann was going to have his ass as it was. But he could not bring himself to go back. Every time he raised his hand to slide the gear shifter out of "park," the idea of having to face any part of it lowered his hand back down to his side.

"Goddammit," he muttered, resting his head against the wheel. "Goddammit!" This time a yell, pounding the dashboard in impotent fury. "Goddammit!"

Slouched in her truck in the far corner of the parking lot, Natasha glanced at the news feed displayed on her phone and noticed that the case was trending. "Police CSI arrested in burning death of teenage girl."

She adjusted her Bluetooth earpiece. Her smartphone lay beside her. On the other line, she could hear the sandpapery noise of Benson scratching his beard while he waited for her to continue.

She said, "Dad used to hit her all the time. She cooked his food the wrong way, which she always did 'cause she couldn't cook, she forgot to buy his cigs. Whatever."

"What did she do when he hit her?"

She scowled against the memories. "Nothing. She cried and said sorry and said she'd do better next time."

"I see."

"When I was nine, he hit her bad, cold-cocked her, and she fell and hit her head, and she died."

"That must have been awful for you."

"Yeah."

"Did he go to jail?"

"Five years. I testified."

"He died not long after he got out, correct?"

"About two years. He was dealing meth again and he got shot 'cause he always carried his drug stash with him. Dumb bastard couldn't do anything right."

Benson changed course. "You must have felt awfully alone."

"My great aunt took me in for the foster money."

"That wasn't what I asked."

Damn it. "Being alone was better. Being alone was easier."

A pause. She could see Benson in her mind, his soft, academic features at odds with the keen intelligence in his eyes. "Did you forgive him for what he did?"

The question would have normally made her erupt, but the madness of the past three days had softened her. "You don't forgive a dog that bit you. You shoot it or you walk away. The fucker died before I could shoot him, so I walked away."

"What did you walk away to?"

"The academy. Richmond. Made detective in record time."

"And Linc?"

She twirled her hair around a finger. "Linc didn't get it."

"Didn't get what?"

"That there's more to life than lost puppies and stolen lawnmowers. We could have moved up together. I tried to help him. And he moves back here and marries his ex from high school. I mean, Jesus Christ."

Benson paused again. "Did any of those things make you happy?"

He had a knack for asking questions that made her think. It was what she hated about him most. "Nothing that's supposed to make you happy ever does."

His tone became a little brighter and softer. "I think you're making progress, Natasha."

Progress.

Toward what?

Her timer pinged. She said nothing. Benson asked, "Is there anything else you want to talk about?"

Like the fact that I'm hallucinating every night?

Like the fact that I'm scared I'm losing my mind?

She suddenly realized that she was holding her badge in her hand. It sparkled as the sunlight bounced off it in turbid patterns. Its wallet was cheap, but the leather creaked and smelled rich with newness just the same.

Do not tell him.

She traced a finger over the ridges and valleys across the brass emblem that spelled out her career's last chance.

Do not tell him. If you do, it will get back to McGann, and that will be the end.

"Natasha?"

She snapped the wallet shut. "I'll talk to you next week."

McGann sat at his desk and desperately craved a nip of scotch.

On his monitor, he watched a replay of the press conference that had taken place an hour ago. The Wright's Crossing police department had no media room, so they'd set up a podium and folding chairs in the lobby of City Hall. The sun shone through large glass windows, but the space was still too small for the purpose. It made the number of reporters seem larger than it was. McGann watched himself at the podium. Briggs stood behind him to his right. Her eyes, her expression were a little too relaxed – her shrink had told him about the pills – but she knew how to hold herself in front of a camera, unlike Meyers, who teetered and fidgeted beside her. McGann had put Dudley on his left to put another uniform in the shot besides his own, but now he regretted it. The fat numbnuts preened like a show horse.

The reporters included two from the Richmond TV stations and one each from Norfolk and Charlottesville; the cable stations would buy the footage from one of them. There were a few reporters from the newspapers around the area, two bloggers, Merriman of course, but no one from DC or the wire services.

A pretty low turnout for a murdered white girl. It would have been impossible to squash the story completely, but Randolph had done a good job of minimizing it.

He watched himself read through his prepared remarks – praise for Briggs and Meyers, example of good teamwork and police work, etc. McGann felt sweat glisten on his forehead, just as it had during the press conference.

It's alright. All be over soon. Burn that damn house down myself and that will be that.

He dry-swallowed an antacid tablet and yearned for that nip.

He watched himself take the first question from the doll-baby who fronted one of the Richmond stations. "Chief McGann, seeing as the murder was committed by an employee of the police department, will the state be doing any kind of follow-up investigation?"

He'd been expecting that one. "That is possible, and if they decide to do so, they will get our full cooperation." They wouldn't, though. Randolph had seen to that, too.

Next was a scruffy guy wearing a hippie-weave shirt, one of the bloggers. "Mister McGann, some people are claiming that this investigation was worked harder than the one into the death of Shaquanna Washington last year. Can you comment on that?"

"Some people" meaning you and your friends, you little prick. But the kid had chosen the wrong case to poke him with. McGann smiled as he watched himself reply, "You may

remember that we caught her murderer as well, sir. Just took us a little longer because we didn't have Detective Briggs with us, yet." A few soft chuckles throughout the room. McGann noticed a subtle scowl from Meyers, then he noticed Briggs give the man a furtive glance. He'd heard about the screaming match between the two of them.

Forget it. She caught Eddie, now all this can go away.

He watched himself field several more questions, one about permissive parenting ("Parents can't lock their kids inside all day long"), another about how Eddie had managed to get hired in the first place ("He passed the psychological screening at the time, and I think his family, his church, his friends are all as shocked as we are by this"). Then, unable to put it off any longer, he had called on Merriman. He remembered how the raw knot in his stomach had tightened another twist, for if anyone was going to go for the throat, it would be Merriman.

But Merriman didn't. "My question is for Detective Briggs, if that's alright. Officer Briggs," he asked with a lighthearted tone to his voice, "were you hoping for an easier caseload when you signed up for a small town police force?"

McGann watched Briggs smile amid another low murmur of laughter around the room, approaching the podium as he stepped aside. She replied, "You've got to take the cases the boss gives you, I guess," with a wry look his way as the laughter increased. The woman was good, no doubt about it.

He clicked off the video, turned off the monitor, and sat for a moment in silence. The rest of the questions had gone easy. No one had asked about what else had happened in that house.

Home free.

For the first time in days, he allowed himself to breathe easy.

Natasha hadn't set out to find a bar. She had taken a road almost at random, hoping she could drive fast enough to disburse the oppressiveness of both the heat and her mood. But less than a mile past the county line she saw it, a half burned-out neon sign that announced, "Floyd's Tavern". Inside she'd found a rough-cut, sticky table dive that felt like coming home again.

Sequestered in a booth toward the back, she drained the last of a scotch on the rocks, the good, cheap, plastic-bottle stuff that went down her throat like mouthwash. She waved the glass at a husky, tattooed waitress. The waitress squinted at her. "You drivin'?"

Natasha's reply was a cold look. The waitress took the glass and retreated.

"Still making friends wherever you go." Linc slid into the seat across from her. He had to speak up to be heard above the outlaw-country music that blared and fuzzed through a worn sound system.

She replied, "Still pushing your luck wherever you can." A few of the bar's other patrons glanced warily at them over their pool cues. "Didn't think this was your kind of place."

"Yeah, I'm usually a wine and cheese man, huh. Saw your truck outside. So, how's it feel?"

A new drink appeared before her. Linc shook his head "no" at the question on the waitress's face, while Natasha sipped, winced at the pleasant burn. "How's what feel?"

His eyes narrowed. "You drunk?"

"Getting there."

His smile clouded. "You just broke the biggest case the town's had in twenty years."

"Your case. I broke your case. You don't have to sit there and Guy-smiley me if you really want to just punch me in the face."

His expression and his tone flattened. "I'm doing the

best I can, okay?" She recognized that tone, that expression. It had been the precursor to every fight they'd ever had, back in the day, and another tussle with Linc was the last thing she needed, or wanted.

"I'm sorry. I'm sorry. I know you are. I don't even know why I said that." She rubbed her hand over her face, but discovered her fingers moved with a dull lethargy and didn't register the contact all that well. *Shit, how many have I had?* A clock on the wall said eight-thirty, still early, but she wasn't sure when she'd gotten here.

Thankfully, Linc exhaled his ire and peace was restored. "Nat, point is, you did it. You're back."

"Yeah." she traced a pattern in the wet circle of condensation left by the glass. "Back. To normal."

He was silent for a moment, just looking at her in that way he had, like he knew everything and nothing about her. "Okay, what?"

Where the hell did you go when you were supposed to be helping me work this case?

Why do I feel like you're falling apart worse than me?

Instead, she said, "He didn't sleep."

"Do what, now?"

"Eddie. He didn't put his head down on the table and sleep while he was waiting for me. He didn't pull his arms into his shirt, didn't hunch over. He didn't withdraw. He looked me in the eye when he answered my questions."

"So he's a good bullshitter. I play poker with him, I could have told you that."

"We searched his house. His computer. His porn collection. What did we find that pointed to this kind of escalation? You saw him at the crime scene. He was surprised when he saw that car. He puked when he heard she was burned alive. Jesus, even the way he cried when I arrested him."

"You think he's the first person to pull the tears, cry 'I didn't do it, I didn't do it'?"

She set her glass down on the scuffed table with an

ominous *thump*. "I know the difference between guilt and grief." Her temple throbbed. She grimaced at the pain, but couldn't stop herself from touching it. She softened. "He said he was sorry."

"Sorry?"

"For attacking me. He said he was sorry. And he was."

Linc became quiet. The aroma of cigarettes and sweat, the music on the tinny sound system, all seemed to intensify in the gap left by his silence. Finally, gently, he asked, "You remember that scene we worked, the banker, Clendarin?"

"Clendenin."

"Yeah. Him. He didn't even have a porn collection. He had two kids who thought he was the best daddy ever, and a boss who just made him employee of the year. And then what he did to his wife? His kids?"

She nodded.

"He was sorry, too. Cried like a baby."

She took another swig to help dull the memory.

"The problem is," Linc said, "It's still all about good versus evil with you." He reached out a rough bear-paw hand and closed it over hers. "Nat, there's only a few really evil people in this world. But there's lots of regular people who are just one or two bad days away from doing some really evil things."

He was not a handsome man, but the earnestness in his eyes was captivating. She wrapped her other hand around his. "I'm glad I'm here, too. I'm glad I came."

She knew it was a mistake to say it, to touch him, but the familiar feeling that moved through her as their hands touched, flowing past her ragged drunk and terrified loneliness, was a life ring thrown to a drowning woman.

After an awkward moment, while a fight broke out nearby that neither of them noticed, he said, "You've had a few."

She told herself, *don't do it*.

"Yes, Mom, I've had a few."
"You… want me to drive you back?"
Don't do it. Don't do it.
"Yes," she said. "I want that."

She fumbled with the keys, his urgency hot behind her, making her clumsy. She shoved the door open and it knocked against the wall with a bang. She swiped a hand over the general area of the light switches and managed to snag one. The living room, in all its drab glory, lit up.

They stumbled past the kitchen area into the living room, grappled in a horny, desperate clinch.

Oh God.

Her body wept with the wanting of him as she felt his powerful arms around her. The musky smell of his sweat charged her animal senses. Her kisses sought to devour him. With a shrug, her jacket was gone. They each took a frantic moment to free themselves from their shirts.

Oh God Oh God.

She felt her back come to rest against the cushions of the couch, felt him fumbling with her bra clasp (he'd never had the knack), and yanked it off to save him the trouble. Her body boiled with the pleasure of his tongue rasping against her nipples.

"Linc." It was a word between a sob and a prayer. "Linc."

They lay spooning on the couch, Linc behind her. She felt his skin, sticky with sweat, cling to hers. She marveled at the sensation of his soft breath in her hair. She wriggled backwards to snuggle closer, felt the world glow.

His voice, languid and warm, asked, "You trying to squash me?"

She giggled. "Trying to get comfortable around your

damn gut."

"Get a bigger couch." The room was a war zone of scattered clothing, throw pillows tossed in every direction. The coffee table had ended up on its side.

For a moment, her euphoria clouded. *You can't do this. This should not have happened. This has to end.*

But oh God, not yet. Not yet.

She felt the rise and fall of his chest against her back lull her into a half-doze. She murmured, "You should be pissed at me."

"Why?"

"I stole your case."

"You helped me get over it."

"So we're even, huh?"

"'Least until I'm ready for round two."

"You are terrible. Terrible."

"You bring out the best in me." He kissed the back of her head through the folds of her hair. "So, what are you gonna do for your second week? Find the Wright Creek Killer?"

"Mmmm." She nuzzled his arm in languorous bliss. "Maybe I'll just solve the other case from that house."

Ever so slightly, his body tensed, his breathing shortened. "What other case?"

"That witness said there was another case from that house."

His body relaxed and he snorted a half-laugh. "Oh yeah, that."

"So what happened?"

"What happened? Guy killed himself. Open and shut."

"Did you work it?"

"I was still a uniform, just helped work the scene. McGann had the case."

"McGann had the case?"

His shoulders twitched in a shrug. "Everyone else was busy. Wasn't a lot to do, anyway. Victim hung

9:13

himself."

"Open and shut."

"Yeah."

"Wonder why Merriman doesn't think so."

He sighed, but it did not sound quite right to her. "You're gonna find stuff out about Merriman."

She drifted for a moment, then said drowsily, "It's just funny nobody told me the suicide was a cop."

"Did it make a difference?"

"No...just funny."

"Funny." He gave the nape of her neck a gentle nibble that sent a bolt of pleasure up and down her body, "What's funny is, you're starting to sound way too much like a cop."

She cooed. "You weren't really just driving by that bar, were you?"

She could feel his smile in the way it moved in her hair. "You're the detective, you tell me."

She wriggled around to face him, to feel the pleasure of him again, and saw the minute hand on the nearby wall clock as it landed on 9:13.

The living room's overhead light was still the only one on, and it blinked off, plunging the room into near-darkness.

Oh, no.

Her ardor evaporated. She sat bolt upright, her shoulder knocking Linc in the nose. "Ow, Jesus, Nat, what –"

"The lights." It was all she could think to say. *Again. Happening again. The same time. Oh Jesus, Oh Jesus.*

"The light's off. It's okay." Linc awkwardly raised himself up beside her. Still in the groove, he purred, "Wouldn't be the first time we did it in the dark." He bent to kiss her neck again.

"Don't." She stood, naked, as fear-adrenaline simmered under her skin. *Something's going to happen. Something's going to happen.* "I, we need... some light in here."

Linc gaped, his puzzlement quickly hardening into annoyance. "Nat, what the hell does –"

"I just need some light!"

She could see him struggle through his hormones for patience. But he stood with a sigh, a fine erection drooping, and asked, "You got a flashlight? A lantern?"

"Over there." There was just enough moonlight filtering through the windows to outline a stack of moving boxes shoved against the wall.

"Great." Any other night, it would have been comical to watch him stumble across the room stark naked, knock his shin against a chair and cuss, finally find his way to the stack of boxes as she followed a few paces behind. Any other night.

He ripped off the packing tape from a box marked "Utility." She watched as he rooted around, shoved aside some garden tools and a length of chain, produced a camp lantern. She released a pent-up breath as the lantern flickered to life. He asked, "You figure this will do the –"

And the chain – *the chain!* – leaped from the box and wrapped around Linc's neck like a snake!

Natasha shrieked. She staggered backwards, felt too late the upended coffee table and fell back, awkwardly landing between table and couch, pain flaring in her elbow, scraping against the backs of her legs. *Oh my God Oh my God Oh my God*

Linc struggled, gurgled with fear as he desperately fought to break the chain's hold, but it gripped his throat and constricted like a python. He thrashed in panic, his horrifying visage winking in and out of the oily shadows cast by the lantern. She watched his face turn red, then purple, then blue. His terrified eyes pleaded with her as he lurched about the room in a macabre waltz of death. He fell to his knees.

Even over her own screams she heard the crackle of breaking bone as the chain crushed his throat. He

9:13

slumped to the floor.

She didn't need to check to know that he was dead.

She stood over him, twitching and shuddering as the horror and fear boiled within her, seeking escape. She heard her voice, a low, animal noise of despair. "Linc," she heard it say. "Linc."

She could not move backward or forward. Finally, she knelt, reached out to pull the chain away and THE CORPSE OPENED ITS EYES.

She shrieked anew as the thing that had been Linc somehow stood, moving with inhuman lurches and jerks, its head lolling at an obscene angle on its shattered neck. She stumbled, narrowly missing the coffee table this time, but felt her feet tangle in her own discarded shirt. She went down again, knocking her cheek against the edge of the couch.

The thing regarded her with bottomless dead eyes, and followed.

Her voice was a ragged wail as she floundered backward from Linc's advancing corpse. She stumbled into the kitchen, slammed into the refrigerator. Stars exploded in her head, and by the time she had collected herself, it was upon her.

The horrible dead face was inches from hers. It looked at her, eyes focused intently from a head that dangled from its ruined neck.

The thing gurgled, "Are…You…Sorry…"

She screamed. And screamed.

And in an instant, it was gone, and Natasha found herself huddled on the kitchen floor, her naked back cold against the metal door of the fridge, and Linc standing before her, unharmed. He gawked in silent horror, his face pale and drawn. His mouth moved, but he didn't make a sound.

Finally, he turned, grabbed up his scattered clothes, clutched them to his chest as he hurried toward the door to the garage. Natasha, shivering on the kitchen floor, heard the door slam, then a minute later, the rev of a car engine, the squawk of rubber on pavement. The engine noise dwindled, and the room was bathed in a terrible silence.

She lay on the kitchen floor for the rest of the night. During her more lucid moments, she found herself calling for someone who'd been a stranger for a long time.

"God. Oh, God. Oh, God."

THE FIFTH DAY

What is happening to me?

She had gotten nothing that resembled sleep. Her years of working police hours were the only thing that now kept her functional.

She sat at her cubicle, her fingers feeling along the pits and scratches of the ancient desk top, her mind sandpaper raw, her eyes burning with exhaustion.

What is happening to me?

All night she had waited for the horrors to return, but they hadn't. What did it mean? Her thoughts struggled through the tar of her fatigue, trying to coalesce into the truth that eluded her.

What is happening to me?
What?
Stop it. Stop thinking like a little bitch.
Think like a cop.

She grabbed a pen and her notepad, and gazed at the blank paper for a full minute.

She'd learned an important lesson when she was young, when they moved from Ohio to Virginia to be closer to Daddy's family because Ma was on the outs with hers. Being closer to his people had brought out a whole new kind of meanness in Daddy. He started leaving bruises on Ma, deep ones that kept her in bed when she should have gone to work. But Daddy's people, led by terrible old Granny Rose, had refused to believe, had accused Ma of lies. No one had seen him do it, they said, and thus it could be denied, and to family and the cops and everyone else it was not real. But then Ma had died, and Natasha had found her voice, had stood up in court and spoken aloud the terrible things Daddy had done. She had spoken of them and made them real, and the very world had shattered and shifted and changed.

Once she wrote it down, the page would speak it back to her, and it would become real and could never again be ignored.

Finally, she wrote, at the top, "What is happening?" Below that, "#1 - I am going nuts."

With an even greater effort, she wrote, "#2 - I am being" – she had to almost force her hand to write the word – "haunted."

Under that, she wrote, "What do I know?"

She listed the facts, as she knew them, the pieces of a gruesome puzzle. "Every night – shortly after 9pm (9:13?)" – "Young Woman – thin, dirty, pissed" – "Blood" – "Chain" – "Are you sorry".

Every night. Are you sorry.

The realization hit her like a slap.

She flipped through her notebook, ignored a "Mornin'," from a passing coworker, found the notes from her interview with Denise Randolph. "Attacked" – "Same time every night – 9pm a little after" – "Grace called it 'she'."

She flipped to her notes from the interview with Andy Wagner. "attacked by a 'demon'" – "Nightmares while still awake" – "Worse every night."

It made sense, now. She reviewed Grace's videos, saw with new eyes the escalation of Grace's fear and desperation. She rested her head in her hand. "This is crazy," she said. "This is fucking crazy."

"I'm not crazy." Natasha jerked her head up as Grace sobbed onscreen. "I'm not crazy. I'm not."

Natasha stopped the video. *And neither am I.*

Grace had told Andy that the attacks began Sunday night.

The night after she visited the dead house.

The gray-haired desk officer in the file room used a hand missing its last two fingers to point Natasha toward an ancient desktop computer, complete with a boxy CRT monitor. It was the case file index, and it was as good a place to start as any.

She reached for the mouse, found nothing, and heard the desk officer snicker. "Gets everybody the first time," he said. "Just hit a key and it'll turn on."

The machine woke from sleep, revealing an old DOS-type numbered menu. She groaned inwardly and chose the "Complainant Name" option and typed in, "Randolph, Grace." The case file number for the current case appeared, but nothing else.

She tried by address. "Williamson Road, 1680." Two file numbers appeared this time, "Randolph, Grace," and "Salyers, Glen." She scribbled the second file number down on a file request slip plucked from a nearby stack, then crossed the short distance to the counter and handed it to the desk officer (the name tag read, "B. Morse"). She couldn't help but stare as he clasped it between a thumb and the remaining fingers on his injured hand.

B. Morse donned a pair of antiquated, Coke bottle-thick glasses that distorted his eyes into funhouse mirror orbs. He squinted at the file request slip, then looked up at her. Even through the distortion of the lenses, his eyes were not kind. "Mind telling me what you want with this one?"

She replied, matter-of-factly, "Follow-up."

His mouth moved in a subtle, silent rhythm, as if he were actually chewing over her answer. Finally, he replied, "I've got a few in line ahead of you, have it ready in a half-hour."

It was a lie and that was obvious. But Natasha turned and walked back toward the staircase that would take her up to her cubicle, feeling Morse's cold, distorted eyes on her back.

She had only been back at her desk for a minute when her phone blooped. The caller ID read, "R. McGann." Before she could say a word, the voice on the other end said, "I need to speak with you, Detective."

McGann was in sync with his tightly-wound office as she sat fidgeting before him. "Background research on a closed case, Detective?"

Her fatigue-addled mind kept focusing on random things – the black hairs on the back of his hand as he clutched a fancy pen, the burbling of the fish tank, the dust on the generic commendation plaques that graced the wall behind him. She struggled to stay sharp. "It's a... thing I do, sir. Trying to get a feel for the territory." *Christ, that was lame.* "Do you mind if I ask you one or two questions about the previous case?"

The hand tensed around the pen, but he replied, "Go on."

"Right. Well..." *Get it together, Briggs, for fuck's sake.* "The victim, Glen Salyers. Could you tell me about him?"

McGann's expression stiffened into a scowl. It was her cue to apologize, to stop asking questions and leave him be, but she remained silent. Finally, he relented. "Glen Salyers grew up around here. He was a state trooper for about twenty years, moved back to town a few years ago, right after his wife passed away. Cancer."

"Did you know him?"

"We were friends in high school. He joined the army, I joined the navy, we lost touch until he moved back. Now if that's all —"

"He had a daughter, is that right?"

"Yes. He had a daughter."

"Crystal."

"Yes."

"She ran away from home, as I understand it?"

A terse nod.

"How... old was she?"

"Sixteen. She was a troublemaker. A few months after she left, he hanged himself in the basement with a length of chain."

A chain. She felt a surge of foreboding, a dry constriction in her throat.

"A chain? He used a chain?"

But McGann had lost whatever patience he'd had. He rose, imperious. "Detective Briggs, is this how you kissed ass at your last job? Trying to solve other people's closed cases?"

"No. No, sir, I'm just —"

"This does not impress me. This is the last time we will talk about a case that has not been assigned to you. Am I understood?"

She resisted the urge to scurry from the room, tried to keep her body language smooth as she stood. "Yes, sir. Understood."

"I'll tell the file room to cancel your request."

"Yes, sir. Of course." She left without another word. He did not sit back down until she was through the door.

She sat at her desk, nursing her wounded pride and trying to wake herself up with a second cup of harsh cop coffee, and suddenly noticed that the cubicle next to hers was still empty. She asked, "Where's Linc?" to a uniform walking past, regretted it an instant later when she realized the uniform was Dudley.

He replied, "Called in sick," but the smirk he said it with filled her with unease.

"Sick?"

"Picked up something last night. I figured you'd know."

"I have no idea what he did last night."

With a snide chuckle, he replied, "That ain't what I heard," as he strutted away.

McGann sat at his desk, clasped and unclasped his hands. He would have liked to convince himself that the roiling in his stomach was from anger instead of fear.

They'd called her the pit bull. Meyers had told him that. They'd been right to.

Why, for Christ's sake? What the hell was she looking for, going into that case? Was she talking to Merriman?

He shook his head. She wasn't the type to talk to reporters.

So why?
She'll let it go. I warned her off, she'll let it go.
No, she won't.
She won't.

Natasha's car screeched to a halt in front of Linc's house, a sedate split-level with a one-car garage and overgrown shrubs. Linc's car sat in the driveway. The garage door was closed. The neighborhood was quiet, most of its residents no doubt at work. She was out of her car and at the front door in seconds.

She tried to control her agitation, knocked softly the first few times, pressed the doorbell gently twice, before giving up and hammering on both. There was no answer. The house had no porch and the heat of the midday sun felt rough on her face.

She thought for a moment and walked to Linc's car. She smiled in satisfaction when she discovered he still never bothered to lock it, reached in and pressed the garage door opener clipped to the sun visor. The garage door slowly trundled open. There was no car inside. Gina wasn't home.

She entered the garage and closed the garage door; no sense in any nearby stay-at-home moms getting suspicious. She smelled car tires, oil, fertilizer. The door from the garage to the house was unlocked.

She entered a tidy kitchen, the formica counter dominated by stainless steel appliances. The fridge door hung wide open and the unit sounded a soft beep-beep-beep of warning as the compressor grumbled. She closed the fridge door and moved into the living room, her ears ringing in the quiet.

She found what she was looking for amid cheap furniture and an expensive television. Linc slumped in an overstuffed easy chair, an empty whiskey bottle resting on the floor but still half-clutched in his limp hand. He was dressed in the clothes he'd worn yesterday, hadn't even bothered to take off his shoes. His snores were soft and wet.

She'd come prepared for this. She raised the pitcher of cold water she'd brought from the kitchen, and sent its contents sloshing into his face. He spluttered, cursed, moaned, and she could see he was still very drunk on top of being very hung over. "Fuck!" He swatted at the water dripping off his face like it was a swarm of bees. "Fuck!" Water soaked his shirt, pooled in his crotch. He blinked at her, and after a long moment, registered her presence. "Fuck. Goddamn, what. What're you doing?"

She tossed the pitcher aside, stood over him in bitter vexation. "What the fuck do you think? What is wrong with you?"

He groaned. "Don't shout." He scrubbed at his face

with his hands.

"Do you know what people are saying? Do you? What they're saying about us?"

"She left."

His words yanked the rug out from under her. *Oh, shit.*

He held his head in his hands, tilted it this way and that as if trying to find some way of holding it that didn't hurt. "Someone saw me driving you home, called her and told her about it."

"Dudley?"

He shook his head and groaned again with the pain of it. "Jesus, Nat, it's a small town. Coulda been anybody. They told Gina and she told everyone else."

"Oh."

"She's gone. Lawyer, whole nine yards."

"Oh."

She suddenly felt full of useless energy. She perched on the arm of a nearby sofa, folded and unfolded her hands. Linc said, "So here we are."

"Yeah." She was desperate to fill the silence. "You… want me to talk to her?"

He blurted a laugh and winced at the pain it caused. A moment later, he added, "It's not the first time I've fucked around. No surprise there, huh."

If not for the horrors of the past three nights and the certainty that more was in store for her, she might have sat there all day, growing sore resting against the sofa arm's flimsy padding, paralyzed with shame. Instead, she said, "Linc, I need your help."

But he was already nodding off, fading back into drunken slumber. "Tell her I'm sorry," he mumbled. "I'm sorry."

She knew from experience he wouldn't be up and about until the end of the day. *God knows what McGann will say.* But that wasn't her problem right now.

She needed to leave. But for a while she sat and

watched him.

Then she stood, pressed a tender kiss to his forehead, and walked out.

No one seemed to notice that she had been out, and for that she said a silent prayer of thanks. Balancing on her off-kilter chair, she woke her laptop from sleep.

The *Colvin County Times* website took time to load, its homepage busy with flickering ads that took up a good two thirds of the screen. The search function, though, worked well enough. She typed in "Salyers 1680 Williamson Road" and was presented with a jumble of links to different articles.

The first link: "Local Police Officer's Death a Suicide." The article included a photograph of Glen Salyers, taken from his time as a state trooper. His face was squared-jawed and sharp-angled, with piercing eyes that showed not a trace of warmth. She shuddered and was surprised at herself.

The next link: "Father of Missing Girl Found Dead." The same photo graced the article. Glen Salyers had been found by a fellow officer, the article claimed, after failing to report to work that morning. The details were sparse. McGann had no doubt kept a tight lid on the case. The article was dated almost exactly a year and a half before today's date.

She tried the next link, which turned out to be a small, back-page follow up article: "Runaway Assistance Group Has No Information on Local Girl." That would be the daughter, Crystal. *She was a troublemaker*, McGann had said, *a few months after she left, he hanged himself in the basement with a length of chain.* It had been more like seven months, based on when the article claimed she had first run away.

Glen Salyers' daughter runs away from home. Seven months later he hangs himself. McGann handles the case, it's ruled it a suicide. Open and shut.

But she knew something was missing. Even as her thoughts struggled through the sludge of her fatigue and her trauma, her cop instincts were still intact, ringing in her ears.

And as she clicked on the next link, she discovered just how right her instincts were.

She clamped a hand to her mouth. Her heart rate juttered into high gear. It took several minutes (*in on four, out on eight, in on four, out on eight*) before she could take her eyes away.

The article itself was a straightforward piece of reporting. "Local Teen Missing, Reported as Runaway." But it was the photograph that had seized her with horror, a selfie of a girl in her mid-teens, blue-collar bone structure, hair streak-dyed in an aggressive style, a broad and brilliant smile, eyes that were just as sharp and cold as her father's. The face wasn't as thin as the one she'd seen the night before last, but there was no mistaking it.

It was the face of her tormentor, the horrible specter that haunted her.

She nearly screamed at the sudden prickling sensation that touched her chest, realizing only then that it was the vibrating of her phone in her jacket vest pocket.

The vibration announced a text message. It was from Randall.

GET HERE NOW!

Randall was hunched over his computer when Natasha entered. Without turning, he asked, "Linc supposed to be here?" in a voice that sounded like he'd spent the past hour screaming.

Natasha replied, "No. Just me."

Randall double-clicked on the file he was looking for and turned. His face had a sickly pale cast. "This shit is not pretty."

"I've probably seen worse."

"Then I pity you."

Onscreen, a jagged explosion of pixels morphed into a familiar image.

Natasha gaped.

It was the video of Grace, filthy and sobbing in the basement of the house, the very same video that had driven her to near-madness two nights ago. "I'm sorry," Grace bawled, exactly as before. "I'm sorry. I'm so sorry. Please forgive me. Please…"

But the absolution that Grace begged for was not forthcoming. The video continued. The girl bowed her head, gave a strangled moan, an animal wail of despair. Her body shook with misery.

The image veered topsy-turvy for a moment, as Grace set the phone down so she could use both hands to reach for something in the darkness. When Natasha finally saw the object that the wretched girl lifted from the floor, she had to grip the back of Randall's chair to steady herself.

It was the gas can.

The can was full, and Grace was well-soaked by the time she was done. She tossed the can aside and picked up the phone, brought it closer to her. Gasoline dripped from her hair, glistened on her skin in the phone camera's light. In her other hand, she now held a lighter.

Grace whimpered, "Sinners must burn."

There was only a moment when Natasha could see the flames surge across the screen, for Grace reflexively clutched the phone to her chest. But the WHUMP of the ignition, the sizzle of the flames, were easy to hear. Natasha felt her throat burn with bile as she listened to Grace's screams of agony. It took time for them to quiet.

Randall sat with his face in his trembling hands. "That's it."

Natasha trembled also, but for different reasons. "Randall, do you swear to me you just finished this file this morning?"

"Why no, Detective, I finished it last night and had the guys over to watch it a few times. Jesus, of course I finished it this morning." His ire was spent quickly. He hugged his skinny arms around himself and rocked slightly in his chair. "Jesus. Jesus Christ. Why did she do it? Why?"

Natasha said nothing. But the answer to his question was clear enough to her.

Because it was the only way out.

Natasha was already back at her desk when the thought struck her. She picked up the desk phone and dialed. The line picked up and the voice on the other end said, "A-V."

"Randall?"

His voice was still unsteady. "Yeah?"

"Half a joint followed by a shot of whiskey will take the edge off for you, but no more than that or you'll be worse off than before." She decided to add, "And none of that flavored bitch whiskey, either, I'm talking the real deal."

There was silence. Then Randall croaked, "Thanks." A moment later, he added, "I never want your job." And the line went dead.

She breathed deep, tried to focus, to wrap her tired mind around what she had seen. But at that moment, the phone rang. She bit back a curse and yanked the phone from its cradle. "Investigations, Detective Briggs."

"Got one for you on Chestnut Street, Detective." It was the dispatcher, a pock-faced woman whose name Natasha had forgotten. "Lady says her lawnmower got stolen."

She could have concocted an excuse to throw the

case to a uniform, but she sensed that it was better to be in motion. She was still half in a daze as she shut the door of her truck and punched the address into her GPS. Chestnut was a long cross street that ran east to west; the GPS chose nearby Liberty Street, which ran north-south, to take her there. Her truck was only a four-banger, and the engine labored as she cranked the air conditioning before pulling out.

She was halfway up Liberty when she passed a rundown retail strip that included a bar, a payday loan company doing a brisk business, and a former hair salon with a "for rent" sign in the window. She only glanced at the sad trio of businesses as she passed, but it was enough to give her a hollow feeling in the pit of her stomach, a bleak sensation of déjà vu. She blinked and found her hands clenching the steering wheel like a vise. She cursed herself for her weakness but was not surprised by it.

Why did I do this?
Why did I come here?

Back when she'd been growing up, there were no such thing as payday lenders. But bars and beauty parlors? They had been everywhere, in every town Daddy had ever dragged them to. Beauty parlors to help put a pretty gloss on your shitty life. Bars to help you forget, once the gloss wore off. The economic foundation of poor towns the world over.

She'd seen her father only once after he'd gotten out of jail. She'd been working the late shift at the Gas-N-Go one Saturday night, trying to finish her math homework between customers. She looked up from her book and there he was, a little thinner, a touch of gray in his beard. "Girl," he said.

She closed the book with careful slowness, adrenaline surging, her mind suddenly hyper-aware of his distance from her, her reach to the emergency button and the baseball bat the manager kept under the counter. "Daddy."

"Think about me?"

"Not really."

His black eyes appraised her; they still shone with their dull, ever-present malice. "Heard you're gonna be a big city cop." Of course he knew. Her cousin Misty had noticed the "law enforcement careers" pamphlet sticking out of Natasha's history textbook, and the next day everybody knew.

"Thinkin' about it."

The old monster smiled with something that might have been genuine affection, shook his head and said, "Girl, you'll never get away from this place." And he'd casually picked up a twelve-pack of beer and left without paying for it, and she'd never seen him again.

She'd sworn to herself that very night that once she left, she'd never again end up in another town like that one.

A town like this one.

She reached the intersection with Chestnut, signaled to turn right. She blinked her tired eyes, waited as a few cars drove by. Then she saw the sign in front of her. "Regional Jail, 10 miles."

The jail.

Of course.

Any one of the town's north/south streets could have gotten her to Chestnut, and yet she'd ended up on the one that pointed her toward a possible answer, the chance to find the way out. Moments like these were almost enough to make her believe in God.

She cut off her turn signal and continued north.

Eddie sat stone-still on his bunk, thinking of ways to kill himself.

They'd put him in solitary for his own protection, knowing what happened in the general population blocks to the molesters and killers of teenage girls. So he'd gone to the hole, a closet-sized cell with two books, no TV, and

9:13

23 hours a day locked down. The other guys in this block were the hard cases, and while steel doors kept them at a distance, they found ways to get to him.

"Baby killah! Hey baby killah!"

"Best hope they don't send you up to Coffeewood, motherfucker–"

"Rip you up! Rip you UP!"

"—I got a cousin up in Coffeewood, let him know you're comin'!"

"Baby killah! Gonna shank your ass!"

They yelled and hollered and banged against their cell doors. It could go on for hours and the guards didn't stop them.

He thought of ways he might trade his commissary card for a razor blade.

He blinked in surprise as the steel flap in his door opened unexpectedly, and a bull-necked guard bent down and spoke through it, raising his voice above the din. "You got a visitor, Shifflett."

Eddie frowned. "It ain't visiting hours."

The guard gave an awkward, bent-over shrug by way of reply, and Eddie approached the slot, turning his back so his hands could be cuffed for escort. The clamor doubled as he exited the cell, the noise swallowing up the guard's angry reprimands. The fluorescent lighting lent a dishwater-grey cast to the space. The smell, like a locker room full of backed-up toilets, still made him want to gag. The guard muttered, "You sure know how to make friends, don't you, Shifflett," as he led him to the meeting room at the end of the cell block.

Eddie entered the meeting room and gawked at the sight of Detective Briggs. To the guard she said, "You can uncuff him."

Eddie sat at the table across from her, rubbing at his wrists as the guard closed the door and again yelled for quiet as he stood his post outside. Eddie shuddered as the convict in a nearby cell slammed something against his cell door, making a clang that Eddie could feel ripple through him. But the noise finally began to die down.

Briggs said, "I need to talk to you."

Something was wrong, wrong about her, wrong about this meeting. "Ain't my lawyer supposed to be here?"

"I… don't have time to wait for him. I need to talk with you now."

He studied her. Her hair was frowzy. There were dark circles under her eyes. Her clothes were wrinkled and seemed to hang on her differently. The iron confidence she'd used to break him was gone. He sensed he had a newfound power, felt his posture straighten a bit, even smiled a little as he replied, "I don't got anywhere else to be."

This was a relief to her. She took a breath and asked, "Eddie, since you were in that house, have you experienced any… nightmares? Anxiety? Anything… strange?"

For a moment, all he could do was look at her. Then he surprised himself by busting out laughing, big, deep, belly laughs that shook him from top to bottom. "Strange?" he gasped as the guffaws finally died down. "I've been doing a teenage girl who gets her damn self set on fire, I dunno, that sound strange to you?"

She bristled. If she'd had a tail, she'd be lashing it. "Answer my question, Eddie. Have you seen or felt anything… wrong?"

He flared with hostility. "What, like I was using? Now you're gonna make it out like I killed her 'cause I was wasted? You ain't got enough on me?"

"Goddamn it!" She slammed her fist on the table. "Answer my question!"

He couldn't help it, smiled an impish smile. "Feel better now?"

She blinked. The great dee-tective blinked.

She recovered with, "Just answer my question," but the words sounded sloppy and weak.

9:13

The guard opened the door, looked in, uncertain. It was Eddie who told him, "It's okay." But when the door had closed again, he sagged, finding himself already spent. "No, I ain't been seeing things, or hearing things. And I ain't been using. My life sucks enough already."

For some reason, his answer deflated her even more. She rested her forehead against a hand and said, "I see."

"Was I supposed to be seeing something?"

She twirled a strand of hair around a finger. For a minute, it seemed like she had forgotten he was there. Then she looked up and said, more gently this time, "Tell me about you and Grace."

"What does that matter?"

"I need to know."

She did, too, for whatever reason. He knew his lawyer would ream his ass for talking to her without him around, but Eddie didn't want to go back to his cell, and he wanted to talk about Grace.

What the hell? It can't get any worse.

He could hear his voice become far away, like his thoughts. "She said she liked being with me, said I was real when everyone else was fake. Stuff like that. I know how messed up that is, okay? I knew it back then. I ain't stupid." He wiped his eyes. "But... I guess it was nice to hear somebody say it."

He gazed at the scratched and dented surface of the table. "I cared about that girl," he said. "I can't say as I loved her, but I never would have hurt her. I wouldn't have done that."

When he looked up again, Briggs was silently watching him with haunted eyes.

And then she totally blew his mind by saying, "I know, Eddie. I know."

The door opened. The guard appeared, nodded toward the clock on the wall, and Briggs nodded back without a word, and Eddie stood for the guard to re-cuff him. He and the guard waited for a moment, but Briggs was silent. "So," Eddie finally said, "what happens now?"

"That I don't know."

The symphony of jeers and taunts erupted again as the guard led him back to his cell, but now Eddie barely heard it, his mind suddenly frothing with new possibilities, new hope.

She knows. She said she knows.

Why is this happening to me?

It wasn't an expression of self-pity, at least not yet. *Why me? Why not Eddie? Why not Linc?* Was she next going to call Paxton and ask her if she'd been attacked by an angry ghost? Dudley? The firefighters?

She was driving too fast, and the car felt stuffy even with the AC on. She was in desperate need of more coffee, and she'd wasted her time and probably blown the case against Eddie. Her stomach growled and she fumbled in the glove box for a granola bar. She'd acted on impulse going to the jail and now she needed to impose some kind of order on her thoughts, plot her next move more carefully. The dashboard clock read: 4:37. Night would be here soon enough.

She munched the granola bar and decided to deal with the most pressing matter first. Through her phone's hands-free earpiece, she heard the other line pick up.

"Hello?"

"Mrs. Dunbarton?"

"Yes, is this the police?" She pronounced it poe-lease.

"Yes, this is Detective Briggs. I... apologize it's taken so long to get out there, I –"

"Oh, don't worry about it, sweetie. I was just about to call back and say don't bother. My nephew takes things and don't ask, so I figured this time I'd call the cops and put a scare into him."

"Oh. I... guess it must have worked."

The lady cackled. "I thought he was gonna poop himself, bless his heart. Anyway, you have a blessed day."

"Ah, you too." The line went dead. In spite of everything, she had to smile. Not only was she off the hook, but now she had the perfect cover for being out of the station. *Maybe there's someone looking out for me, after all.*

She needed information and there was only one other person she could turn to. Crossing the bridge back into town, she dialed another number. A moment later, "*Colvin County Times*, Chad Merriman speaking."

"Merriman. I'll take you up on that drink."

A surprised pause. "Detective Briggs. Sure, where?"

"Your place."

She set two tall coffees on the desk, slid one of them toward him. "Salted caramel mocha with a shake of cinnamon, as requested."

"You know," Merriman said, "When you said you wanted to have a drink…"

"You must get disappointed a lot."

Merriman's office, one of the three that made up the entire footprint of the *Colvin County Times*, was a hurricane of books, papers, and the bric-a-brac of the reporter's trade. A nearby shelf held a high-end digital camera and a dust-covered microcassette recorder. Notes jotted on fast food napkins were lined up carefully on the assemble-it-yourself credenza behind him. She found herself surprised that the place didn't smell like a reporter's desk; it lacked the usual underlying odors of stale takeout food and sweat. His white button-down shirt was suspiciously free of wrinkles and stains. His stubble and his bitter coffee breath, though, were authentic enough.

Amid the jumble, she absently noted several copies of a book, *Haunted Dominion: Strange Tales of Old Virginia*, by *Chad Merriman*. This guy was full of surprises.

There was little space for her in the gap between his

desk and the glass wall that faced the hallway, and her knees pressed against the front of the desk. He sipped his coffee. "Okay." He looked at her; it was her cue to speak.

"Are you recording this?"

"Should I be?"

"Don't fuck with me, Merriman."

"Detective, I swear on my pure white soul I'm not recording this, video-ing this, I don't have a midget under the desk taking notes. I'm not that guy."

"You're a reporter."

"I'm the one who said you needed friends here, and since you're now jeopardizing all the points you've scored with McGann to have a sit-down with me, I conclude that you've decided I'm right." He nodded toward her coffee. "You ought to drink it before it gets cold. And maybe tell me what you wanted to talk about?"

No sense in dragging this out. "I need to know about 1680 Williamson Road. About Glen and Crystal Salyers."

"I don't suppose I get to ask why."

"No."

Her question didn't seem to surprise him, and that in itself was interesting. "If I may ask, how much do you currently know about Glen Salyers?"

"I know he was a state cop for almost twenty years, he grew up around here, he moved back when his wife died. McGann said his daughter was a troublemaker and that she ran away, and that Salyers hanged himself about seven months later."

He nodded, absently tapping a finger against the side of his coffee cup. "Not bad. You got more out of McGann than I ever did." He leaned forward, his eyes bright and intense. "So, a guy pushes blue and gray on the interstate for twenty-two years, and then, at age fifty-one, leaves the state cops three years shy of retiring at full benefits so he can patrol the graveyard shift in the boondocks for half the pay. That raise any red flags to you?"

She nodded. "So why did he do it?"

"Got a few ideas, the first among them being the number of times he was cited for giving suspects a thumping, and those were just the accusations that stuck. I think it's interesting that he came here about a year after his wife died."

"I don't follow."

"Our boy Glen had some anger issues that go way back. In the army he was an MP until he got a little too rough with a guy he suspected of dealing drugs on base. The guy got a medical discharge and Glen got transferred to a base in Alaska for the rest of his term. That's where he met his wife."

She pondered for a moment. "You think his wife helped keep him from getting out of hand?"

"To some extent, anyway. There were a few domestic calls to their home in Staunton that never resulted in charges."

"You really do have some connections, don't you."

The tapping of Merriman's finger on the coffee cup slowed and stopped. He said, "Something happened. He didn't have his wife anymore to keep him under control. I figure he got out of line like he did in the army, and so he's politely asked to leave the state police." After a moment he added, "Puts the whole idea of his daughter being a 'troublemaker' in a new perspective, doesn't it?"

She considered this. "What kind of troublemaker?"

"Can't really say, no official record, her being a minor. Vandalism, truancy, stuff like that, from what I heard. There was a rumor about a domestic call from the house on Williamson Road, but there's nothing in the official police record. Let's just say it doesn't surprise me that she ran away."

"About that…"

"Nothing to tell. Nothing out of the ordinary, at least. Glen said that he woke up after sleeping off the late shift, discovered she was gone. She wrote a good-bye note, apparently. They checked the bus stations and sent out the bolo alerts and all that. She didn't turn up."

"Open and shut."

"So they say."

It was all exactly the kind of information she'd been hoping for, but something nagged at her. "You've done a lot of homework on a small-town cop who lost his daughter and killed himself. Why?"

The question threw him more than it should have. He swallowed, eyes focused for a moment at a spot on his coffee cup. He swigged, even though she could tell the cup was already empty. He opened his mouth to say something, and then checked himself. Finally, he continued with, "Salyers gets transferred to the day shift. His second or third day, he didn't show up for work, didn't answer his phone. So a patrolman was sent to his house to see what was up."

His phone rang. He let it go to voice mail. "The patrolman was dispatched at 7:17 am. His radio call to report the dead body was at 8:52 am."

"And?"

Merriman's face puckered in irritation. "Don't play me like that, Detective. Even I know it doesn't take an hour and a half for someone to drive to that house, find a dead body, and call it in. Plus, I have it on good authority that Chief McGann was at the scene before the patrolman called into dispatch. And finally," he concluded, thumping his desk with the tip of a finger, "I find it interesting that patrolman Lincoln Meyers got promoted to detective a month after the incident. A position, I might add, he didn't exactly have the resume for."

And when he saw the reaction she was too tired to hide, he remarked drily, "And I can't help but notice that you find it interesting, too."

Natasha sat there, silent, words and times and facts grinding against each other in her mind, trying to find a way to assemble themselves in a way that made sense. *Linc finds the body. Calls McGann before calling in the report? McGann takes the case…*

Slow down. Slow the fuck down.

"When you wrote the articles about Crystal running away, or about Glen Salyers killing himself, did you interview any friends? Relatives?"

"Tried to." He tapped a few keys on his laptop, bringing up what she assumed were his notes. "He has a sister who said she'd shoot me if I ever called back. Nothing from Glen's coworkers, of course. There was a friend of the daughter's I tried to talk to a few times, but I never got anywhere."

"Friend?"

"Yeah." He busied himself with double-clicking first one folder, then another. "Here it is. BFF, from what I gathered. Girl named Andrea Wagner."

Andrea Wagner. It only took a second for the name to register.

Andy.

Merriman had turned to face his laptop, so he didn't notice her mouth falling open in shock. She had collected herself by the time he turned back to her, moving his laptop so she could behold a scanned yearbook picture. The caption read, "Best buds Crystal Salyers and Andy Wagner plan to rock out the summer together." They stood arm-in-arm, Crystal sporting pink and purple streaks in her shoulder-length, dishwater-blonde hair, dressed in an unbuttoned flannel shirt thrown over a sport-cut tank top. She grinned her brilliant, cold smile as Andy, a faded, baggy shadow in worn t-shirt and jeans, did her best to ape Crystal's rock-star pose.

Natasha stood up too quickly and banged her knee against the desk. "I'll be in touch. I owe you one, Merriman."

As she exited, he called after her, "And you better not forget it."

The current receptionist at the Divine Worship Center of Blessed Jesus the Deliverer was a hatchet-faced woman in her fifties, clad in a discount store print dress. "Young Miss Wagner is out ministering to the unfortunate. Can I help you with something?"

Natasha showed her badge. "I need to speak with her right away. Can you call her and tell her to come here?"

The woman's expression remained impenetrable. "I'm afraid I don't have her cell number, dear. I'm just filling in. Would you like to wait for her?"

Natasha felt the buzzing in her temples that told her she was reaching her limit. She spoke slowly and deliberately to keep herself from screaming. "It is very important for me to speak with her now. Can you call the people she's 'ministering' to?"

"I'm afraid I wouldn't know who to call, dear. She didn't give me a list. She's sure to be back in a while, seeing as there's worship tonight."

Natasha said, through gritted teeth, "I'll come back later." She thumped her card on the desk. "Please have her call me immediately. It's very important."

The woman remained unruffled. "I'll be sure to do that, dear."

Natasha turned and left. Had the woman even blinked during their conversation?

Natasha trudged back across the church's parking lot. She tripped on one of the many crumbling potholes and cursed. She'd parked under a spindly tree at the edge of the lot, which cast a precious bit of shade on her truck. She found it only a touch cooler on the inside than in the bristly outside heat. She swigged the last of the coffee she'd brought to Merriman's, grimaced as she swallowed the lukewarm sludge. She rested her head against the headrest.

So now what?

The dashboard clock read: 5:24. There'd been no calls for her, for which she was grateful, but God only knew how long her luck would hold out. She fumed at having to slow down. Without forward motion, she could feel her exhaustion expand, from her bones through her muscles and into her veins, soft and warm and unyielding.

Will it happen again?

Of course it will. But when, exactly? How?

She felt sweat beading on her forehead, her upper lip. She reached for the ignition to start the truck and run the AC, but noticed that the fuel gauge showed less than a quarter tank. "Fuck."

She sighed. *Just suck it up and wait.*

For a moment - *just for a second* - she closed her eyes.

When she opened them again, she found herself splayed awkwardly on her side on the truck's bench seat. The spot on which her head had rested was wet with drool and sticky sweat. She hitched a breath at the twinge in her side as she raised herself up, fighting to clear her mind from the fog of sleep. She blinked, trying to decide which detail to focus on first. There were messages on her phone. Two from dispatch, one from Linc. *Oh, shit.*

Then she noticed other things, and a bolt of panic shot through her.

The parking lot was full. The sun was low. It would be full night in minutes.

The dashboard clock now read: 8:23.

The foyer and hallway were empty, but it was easy to follow the noise toward the double doors past the stairwell. Natasha strode toward the sounds of a blood-and-guts sermon on the other side, fuming at her predicament, cursing herself for her weakness. She heard a wild male voice as she approached. "JEE-zus does not care how Godly we THINK we are! JEE-zus does not care about our INTENTIONS! JEE-zus —"

The sermon, with its chorus of shouted amens and hallelujahs, cut off instantly as Natasha shoved open the door. She came to an abrupt halt. The small sanctuary was full to overflowing, parishioners packed onto rickety pews, some spilling off into the aisle. They watched her with suspicious eyes. She found herself amazed by how many of them were fat. The room stank of mildew and sweat, and for a moment she was painfully transported back to many unhappy Sundays spent in angry saunas just like this one.

She spoke in her best cop tone that did not shout but brooked no dissent. "Andy Wagner."

The portly, sweaty man who could only be "Bishop" Pyle glowered at her from the front stage, his florid face astonished and affronted.

Natasha repeated, "I need to speak with Andy Wagner. Now."

"Miss," said the preacher, tugging at an ill-fitting suit, "We will thank you to wait until the service is over." He said it slowly, like he was talking to someone who didn't understand English. The faces of his flock curdled with judgement.

Natasha brandished her badge. "And I'll thank Andy to come with me before I report you to the fire marshal, and maybe the building inspector, too."

She allowed herself a moment of satisfaction as Andy rose stiffly from the front pew amid the stunned silence. Andy mumbled, "It's okay" to some of the worried faces around her as she trudged up the aisle to where Natasha stood.

The sermon resumed almost the moment the doors clacked shut behind them. "JEE-zus does not care about our EGO, our self-RIGHTEOUSNESS!"

9:13

Natasha observed Andy as the young woman slouched in the passenger side of the truck. She'd traded her flip-flops for a pair of shabby slip-ons, but other than that her outfit could have been the same one she'd worn the previous day. Andy did not look up, her hands clasped in her lap. "So what do you want to know?"

"For starters, I want to know just how much you hate cops."

The young woman's reply was a confused look. "I… I don't follow you, ma'am."

"I've been doing this a long time, Andy. It doesn't just happen that you wouldn't think to tell me about Crystal Salyers."

Alarm flashed across Andy's face at the mention of that name, but it was quickly replaced by a sullen enmity. "No offense, ma'am, but you didn't ask anything about Crystal."

Natasha seethed inwardly. Her hand white-knuckled her pen. "You told me everything you could about your prayer buddy, Grace, and nothing at all about your best friend. Everyone in this town talks about everyone else."

"Well, maybe I don't!" Andy's eyes sparkled with sudden wrath, her voice hard and bitter. "Maybe I don't talk about people. Maybe it just ain't really none of your business, now is it?!"

She locked eyes with Natasha's cop glare for a full ten seconds before she turned away toward the window, folding into herself. Outside, the last pink streaks of dusk were fading. "What do you want?" asked Andy, tears creeping into her voice. "What do you *want*?"

Something in that voice finally pierced Natasha's desperation. *Jesus, what am I doing?* She did a single breathing exercise to steady herself and sat back, chagrined. "Andy," she said, forcing her voice to be gentle, "I'm sorry. I'm sorry. The truth is that I need your help. I need you to tell me about Crystal. It might… help me with Grace's case."

Andy turned back to face her, wary. "I thought you caught the guy that killed Grace."

"It's just... some background I need. It's important." She suddenly thought to rummage behind her seat for a battered box of tissues, handing them to Andy. "Please, tell me."

Andy gazed at her feet, silent. The dashboard clock read, 8:47. When she spoke again, dabbing at her eyes, her voice was soft and far away. "We met at church."

"This church?"

Andy nodded. "It was youth night and I was crying in the bathroom 'cause my dad had just walked out on my mom and I." Her hands had become still. "So Crystal comes in and finds me there, starts talking to me. She told me about how her mom died. She hated church but her dad was making her go. We stayed in the bathroom the whole time, talked about stuff, smoked a cigarette." She broke into the first real smile Natasha had seen on her. "Got the youth counselor all mad at us."

Andy paused to blow her nose. "And we were friends after that. Shared a locker at school. Hung out, you know. I never had a friend like that before her."

Natasha asked, "What was she like?"

Andy smiled again, but the sadness back of it was palpable. "She was wild. She wasn't afraid of anything. She didn't take any shit from the mean girls. She didn't let the boys get a piece of her. People said we were lesbians 'cause the boys couldn't get her and they didn't want me."

Natasha was silent. *Wait for it.*

"But she was so sad. She hated her life."

From the church, the faint sound of singing. Natasha asked, "Why did she hate her life?"

"Because of her father." Andy's face contorted in hatred and grief. "Because of her... *damned* father."

A vague image of Glen Salyers had already formed in Natasha's mind after her talk with Merriman. And as Andy spoke, the image came into bleak and monstrous

9:13

focus…

Natasha has seen many men like Glen Salyers in her career and in her life, and the movie in her mind is rich and detailed.

He is older than the newspaper photo, a few more crags in his face, more gray hairs peppering his crewcut. He walks slowly through the front door of his home, but moves, as always, with purpose. Even now, with all that has been taken from him, he moves from nowhere to nowhere at a march. And silently, he rages.

His job, his real job, his reputation and his honor, gone, taken from him by cowards and thieves. His current job in this podunk shithole, however graciously offered by his old friend McGann, does nothing to console him. He's spent another day arresting shoplifters and penny-ante pot dealers, responding to calls from sly bitches who use domestic complaints to score points against boyfriends and baby-daddies. Stuck in a dead town with a dead wife and a dead life, he prowls his house in a low boil, looking for a reason to erupt. It doesn't take him long to find one.

He is a man who notices the slightest deviation from the standards he lays down, a man who lives in constant fury with a world that mocks his sense of order. Today, like every day, there are plenty of petty challenges to be found. A pair of pink flip-flops carelessly kicked off near the door. A book bag resting tilted on the couch instead of being taken upstairs. A peanut butter-covered knife in the sink. He can feel the bile rise in the back of his throat.

He doesn't drink very often, not a man like him, but at this moment a sip doesn't sound so bad, a tiny break in an otherwise bleak routine. He opens the cabinet high up above the refrigerator. He reaches in almost without looking, for in this house everything is kept in its place.

But the cabinet is empty. His permanent scowl bends in full-fledged wrath.

Down the hallway. Up the creaky steps, taking them fast, his equipment belt thumping in rhythm against his hips, and then through the hallway door closest to the stairs.

Inside, Crystal snores in drunken slumber on her bed, his new bottle of bourbon now half-empty on the nightstand next to her.

He reacts with military swiftness and precision, crossing the room with efficient quiet, carefully screwing the cap back on the bottle. Then, with a practiced hand, he grabs a fistful of Crystal's colorful hair, close to the scalp, and yanks her off the bed.

The movie in Natasha's mind fast-forwards.

The basement is cold and rough and dirty, a hell-place, and Crystal Salyers feels hell once again. She kneels on the concrete floor, facing the back wall, her hands handcuffed to the metal ring that was set into the wall for just this purpose. Her father stands above her, his face a mask of hatred and delight, as he brings a belt down on her back with a CRACK. It's an old Sam Browne cop belt, a heavy wide plank of leather that he keeps handy for times like this, and her body spasms with the pain of the blow.

CRACK. Tears and snot pour down her face, but she dares not cry out; it will only make him hit her more. CRACK. Her body shakes with pain. She hitches in silent sobs. CRACK.

He stops, panting, sweaty-faced, glowing. He asks, "Are you sorry?"

She cringes before him. Other days she might resist for a while, endure another round of blows for the pleasure of a moment's defiance, but not today. "I'm sorry, Daddy," she hitches. "I'm sorry."

But he's not through. Glen Salyers' world is built on structure, order, ritual, and this ritual is not yet played out. He plucks a cigarette lighter off a nearby shelf, the lighter also kept there for just this purpose. He uncuffs his daughter, tosses the lighter to her, and growls, "Sinners must burn."

And what comes next, Crystal does because she has to, because she knows from long and terrible experience that if she does not comply in exactly the way he demands, she will stay cuffed to this wall until she does. She flicks on the flame and holds it under her arm, a spot above the elbow but near the armpit, a place where the burn won't show. She holds it there, gritting her teeth from the red, angry pain, until her father is satisfied.

He turns toward the stairs. She folds into herself on the rough, cold floor, and sobs.

Glen mounts the basement stairs, boiling with elation. Those who do right have been vindicated. Those who do wrong have been punished. For a moment, his daughter's cries are the songs of the angels to him, her misery a balm to his soul.

For a moment all is right in his world again.

"Detective?"

Andy's voice prodded Natasha out of the vision. She found herself back in the truck, back in the now. She breathed in and out. She fought back a wave of visceral sorrow, her understanding of Crystal Salyers deeper than she could have expected or wanted. She noticed that the page in her notebook was still blank. Andy sat slumped beside her, wiping her tear-streaked face with another tissue. "Is that what you want to know?" The young woman's voice sounded tired and small.

The dashboard clock read, 8:59.

Natasha's mind spun on an erratic axis, trying to find every connection at once and finding none. *Don't panic. For Christ's sake, don't panic. You'll see something. It won't last, it won't kill you.*

But she was panicking. She could feel her breathing shorten, pain flare in her stomach.

"Are you sorry"? What does it mean? What am I supposed to be sorry for?

What did I do? Jesus Christ, what did I do?

But the cop in her took control again. "Andy," she asked, successfully keeping the tremor out of her voice, "tell me about when Crystal ran away."

Andy's body language had slowly loosened as she'd spoken about her friend, her posture softening, eye contact increasing. But at that question she instantly retracted. Natasha could hear the tension in her voice when she replied, "There… isn't much to tell, ma'am."

Liar.

"Go on."

"I mean, one day she was gone. She didn't… tell me she was going or anything."

Bullshit.

Natasha could feel her gorge rise as the dashboard clock blinked to 9:06. "She told you nothing. Didn't leave a note. Never called you."

Andy held her hands in her lap, but still could not stop them from their tell-tale fidgeting. "No, ma'am. I guess she… just wanted a fresh start or something."

Natasha felt the last of her patience evaporate with the minutes on the clock. "See, Andy," she said, hearing her voice rise, "here we are again. I get the whole story about Grace, I get nothing about Crystal. I get everything I ever needed to know about what a bastard Crystal's dad was, and I get nothing about the day your best friend ran off." She leaned in, regarded Andy, her eyes hard and angry. "I do not have time for this."

Andy blanched, began to tremble. "Ma'am, I… I can't tell you what I… don't know."

Natasha leaned in, her face now mere inches from Andy's. "She did not run away. I know it. And you do, too."

But she had underestimated Andy. She'd thought the church mouse would break, but instead she saw the young

9:13

woman's eyes suddenly blaze with defiance. Her lips flattened into a sneer, her chin stuck out and almost hit Natasha in the nose. "Well, you wouldn't know much about it, would you?" she hissed. "You fucking cops." And with that, she shoved open the car door and slid out.

Natasha fumbled with her door latch. "I'm not done with you —"

Andy spun on her heel. "You fucking cops. You fucking cops!" Then she was off, running for the church in long, furious strides.

Natasha jumped from the truck to follow, but the church door was already shushing closed, Andy's shadow disappearing around the corner. She hustled across the parking lot, forcing her muscles to move with control, slow-breathing the soupy night air, fighting the rising panic that threatened to choke off her breath. *It's going to happen. It's going to happen.*

The building's weak air conditioning was suddenly taut on her skin. As she crossed the foyer, approaching the right turn toward the hallway to follow Andy, she noticed the wall clock click to 9:13.

When she rounded the corner, things had changed.

Oh, Jesus.

The hallway was deserted. The amens and hallelujahs that had chorused from the sanctuary were gone. Dim stillness. Deathly quiet. The air was cold, pregnant with an ominous energy. The mildewy smell – *any* smell – was gone.

Jesus God.

She could have turned back, could have run from the building and driven away, driven all night, driven as far from this godforsaken place as she could go, but she knew that it would do no good. She crept forward. The floor seemed to absorb the sound of her footfalls. She could hear the blood rushing in her ears, and nothing else.

She startled, jerked with electric swiftness, touched her head. A drop of water. A drop of water had dripped from the fire sprinkler above. There were two other sprinklers in this hallway. Water dripped lethargically from each.

Halfway down the hall, a puddle was forming.

She approached it. Fear thundered from the primitive parts of her mind, saturating her body with adrenaline, but her cop's discipline kept her pace steady and slow. She kept her hand on her gun, even as she knew without knowing that the Glock was useless in this place.

I have to stay in control. I can't let this win. I have to stay in control.

She reached the puddle.

A new droplet of water swelled lazily from the sprinkler, this time darkening to a bloody red.
The droplet fell in slow motion, splashing into the puddle, and the color spread, rippling through the puddle, transforming all of it into the same viscid crimson.

Blood.

The puddle was only two feet across, but the surface shivered and rippled as if it were somehow much deeper, as if something underneath the surface lurked and waited.

God. Oh God.

Survival instincts clamored for her to run, but her muscles would not obey, expanding and contracting of their own accord until she found herself crouched next to the murky pool. The vile smell of the blood filled her nostrils and for a moment she thought she would vomit. In a choked voice she breathed, "Crystal."

And a length of chain burst from the surface of the pool!

The blood sprayed in all directions as the chain, with preternatural power, slithered around Natasha's neck like a snake. Natasha gagged, gurgled in terror as the chain closed its grip. She scrabbled backwards, desperate, her shoes finding little purchase on the blood-slicked floor.

The chain began to pull her back.

She thrashed and twisted like a hooked fish, animal-desperate and doomed, as the force beneath the surface of the pool dragged her inexorably toward it. She wheezed, barely able to breathe, her writhing rapidly depleting her body of oxygen.

A flash before her, a horrible *whoosh* of ignition, and the bloody pool suddenly blazed into a pit of molten fire. The flames reached, danced in the air, undulated toward her. Agony flared as her skin felt the heat. She could not scream. A frail squeak was all that managed to escape her lips.

From the pit, a human figure was rising. Liquid flame dripped from the livid gray skin. Even as Natasha's struggles grew feeble and her vision blurred, the face, the horrible, leering face, was all too familiar.

Natasha gurgled, "Cr.. Cryssstl…"

The dreadful vision of Crystal Salyers smiled. As Natasha felt the last of her strength dissipate, felt the searing heat of the fire blaze across her face as the chain pulled her into the pit, she heard Crystal hiss, *"Sinners must burn."*

And in another instant, it was over. Natasha came to, found herself sprawled on the church hallway floor.
She gulped air as she struggled to stand. Her muscles were like cords of flaccid rubber, her face still stinging from the kiss of the flames, her clothing soaked with slimy sweat.

The service could again be heard, a raucous hymn that Natasha recognized.

Andy stood before her, gaping, stricken.

Natasha turned, every movement causing her used-up muscles to cry out in protest, and staggered down the hallway toward the door.

Linc was puking and screaming when his phone warbled.

Out of reflex, he checked the screen, and when he saw who was calling, he groaned, tried to pull himself together as best he could. He did his best to smooth the hitching in his voice as he answered, "Yes sir?"

McGann snarled, "Are you drunk again?"

Not good... Not good. "I'm... okay." The pressure in his head from the crying and the heaving made it feel like a balloon too full of air.

"Do you know what she's done?"

"Wha-what?"

"Do you know what she's DONE?!"

Natasha was driving down a two-lane side road, halfway to her house, when she felt the last of her strength give out. Her hands went limp and her leg muscles stuttered as she tried to make them work the pedals. She managed to pull off onto a rutted, overgrown track that cut across an open field, stopped the truck, and slowly fell across the truck's bench seat.

She lay in the shadows cast by the moon and couldn't find the strength to weep.

I'm going to die.

Moonlight filtered through the windows, casting dim and eerie shadows as the night insects hummed outside. Occasionally the headlights from a passing car would sweep past, bringing the sad limits of her world into momentary relief. She grasped her phone in a clumsy hand and started to call Benson, but cut off the call after the first ring. What the hell would she say?

I'm going to die.

She had half-believed that the horror would not happen again. She had fully believed that if it did, she could handle it, that she could face the challenge. She wasn't a weepy child of privilege like Grace Randolph. She was Natasha Briggs, the girl – the teenager – the woman, who fought the monsters and always survived.

But I can't survive this.

The hauntings got worse each time. She understood

that now. They got longer, more terrifying, more painful. She had been sure it was all in her mind, and maybe she was right, but what difference did it make? In the ether of her mind, trapped with the revenant of Crystal Salyers, she was utterly defenseless. How do you fight a creature that can make your skin believe it is burning, make your throat believe it is choking, a monster that can tell your body to suffer and your body obeys?

You don't.

It was clear to her now why Grace had gone back to the house. Pushed beyond desperation, Grace had gone there to beg for forgiveness, to pray to the demon god that persecuted her and seek its absolution. But Grace had found none, and Natasha knew that she herself would find none as well. She would suffer until she gave in, until she inflicted on herself the same horrible sentence that the specter of Crystal Salyers had imposed on Grace.

Sinners must burn.

Andy had gone back to the service, kept a pleasant face during fellowship afterward, chuckled off all the concerned questions. She'd told Bishop Pyle she would stay late to finish a few things and would lock up, and soon enough she was alone in the building.

Now she sat at her desk in the dingy outer office. Her hands cast restless shadows in the light of the desk lamp. Her back still murmuring in pain from the offering she had given two days ago, she struggled against the truth.

She had hated Grace Randolph on sight. That was pre-judging of course, and not very Christian of her, but she'd endured taunts and slights from girls like Grace all her growing-up life, she and Crystal both. (Crystal had spat it right back in their faces, of course, wild, amazing Crystal, while Andy huddled in her shadow). Andy remembered her first meeting with Grace, how she'd offered a bottle of water and the girl had asked for a

"Pellegrino," whatever in God's name that was. But then Grace had started talking, and the talking quickly became sobbing.

Andy opened the bottom drawer of her desk. From a hanging folder at the back of the drawer she removed a piece of heavy paper. Trembling, she unfolded it and laid it out on the desk before her.

Crystal.

There was a lot she hadn't told Detective Briggs. Grace had talked all about the "devil" that was tormenting her, had even drawn this picture. Grace was a good artist. She'd captured perfectly the curve of the lip, the slightly flat nose, the wide cheekbones.

What was I supposed to do? Jesus in Heaven, what was I supposed to think?

She fumbled down the hallway, not bothering to turn the lights back on. It would be just her luck someone would notice them and come to see what was going on. She could make out a few dim shapes that she used as landmarks: the water fountain, the fire extinguisher, the huge construction-paper cross taped to the older kids' Sunday School classroom door.

She opened the door of the sanctuary. The room was still imbued with the passion of the night's service; it tingled on her skin.

A single bulb illuminated the cross, providing the room's only light. Andy did her best praying at times like this. God seemed closer in the dark.

She knelt before the altar. When she finally spoke, she did not speak God's name.

"Crystal."

All the tears she had cried had never sated her grief, like the crappy charity food she had to eat when she was young – food you could eat and eat and always still be hungry. But now her sadness was eclipsed by something else, a sense of black dread and unrelenting guilt.

She thought of the voice mail message stored on her

phone. *"Andy, Andy please—"*

"Crystal," she whispered to the empty gloom, "what have I done to you?"

THE SIXTH DAY

Natasha awoke, still sprawled across the seat of her truck. *This is getting to be a thing with me*, she thought, and was surprised at the violence of the laughter that gushed from her, leaving her gasping as she tried to collect herself in the early morning light. Her mouth was dust-dry. She felt sticky and slimy. Pain twanged in her arm and her side as she pushed herself up to a sitting position. The worst of the horrible exhaustion was past, but her muscles felt sluggish and half-spent.

She looked about the overgrown field around her and tried to work out her next move. Her smartphone had ended up in the footwell, and her muscles griped as she bent to retrieve it. The screen read: 6:52.

Focus on the now. Food, shower, clothes. Work out the rest later.

She started the truck and made an awkward three-point turn to avoid disturbing the field as much as she could.

It was only a few minutes later that her house loomed in the windshield, only seconds after that when she saw Linc's car parked in the driveway, Linc climbing from the car and squinting through the last of his own sleep.

Before she knew what she was doing, she had skidded to a halt and leaped from the truck. She wrapped her arms around him, clung to him. She pressed her face against his chest and whimpered, "I have to tell you something crazy, and I really need you to believe me."

Too late, she noticed his rigid posture, his arms held at his sides. She broke away as he asked in a voice thick with reproach, "What the hell have you done?"

His face was ashen. His eyes were bloodshot and shadowed, his smell rancid and wrong. Her heart sinking, she replied, "I could ask the same thing about you."

"You talked with Eddie Shifflett. Without his lawyer there."

She could feel the outrage coming off him in waves. She replied, simply, "Yes."

He looked disappointed in her ready confession. The key to making Linc feel like a man was to make him feel like a cop, and she'd always been worthless at both. But he recovered quickly enough. "Well? I can't wait. I can't *wait* to hear this."

A wave of dizziness washed over her. She leaned against his car, massaging her temples. "Hear what? What the fuck do you want to hear?"

"You had him wrapped up. Wrapped up. This case, this... case! And then you sit down alone with him and tell him you think – no, you tell him you *know* – that he didn't do it."

"He didn't."

"Nat, what the fuck? What the fuck have you done?"

"Linc," she replied slowly, as the smell of him made her stomach turn, "I kind of don't need this right now."

"Oh, bullshit. Bullshit!" He paced in an erratic circle around her. "Screw the evidence. Screw everything. You just don't think he's guilty, so he's not. And you've ruined it. You've ruined everything."

She had endured horrors beyond anything she could have imagined, and this was her reward. Her heart flared with rancor and hurt and there was only one place for it to go. "You want to know what I was doing, Linc?" She felt that familiar edge creep into her voice, raw and dangerous, but she gleefully welcomed it this time, drew power from it as she stepped in front of him to block his pacing. "You know what I was doing, talking to Eddie? My job. I was doing my fucking job."

"Your job. Your job. Your job was to make an arrest!"

"Arrest an innocent man, just because?"

"Because, for God's sake, he did it!"

"He was not there! He did not do it!"

"How!" He spluttered. "How do you know that? You've got nothing. Nothing!"

"You," she hissed, "are the one who's been so fucking desperate for Eddie to be guilty. You and McGann. Why? Was it because you didn't want people to take a second look at that house?"

She watched the color drain from him. He took a step to close the gap between them, standing ramrod straight and chin jutting forward to maximize his slight height advantage. It was a familiar sight, the sign that she'd cut deep. The last time she'd seen it was their final fight before he left for good. "So we're gonna go there, huh? We're really gonna do this." He was gulping his breaths and his voice was hoarse. "You're just smarter than everyone, right? You just don't think he's guilty, so he's not. That's what it is, huh? Huh?"

She locked her gaze with his, unwavering. "Why did you bring me here?" Her voice was a low, husky growl.

"What, what the hell are you talking about?"

"Why did you bring me here? Why? You're getting blackout drunk on company time, your boss doesn't care shit about who's guilty and who's not, you both let the Randolphs push you around. And you knew I wouldn't sit for any of it. You knew it. So why did you bring me here? Why?!"

"I brought you here to try and help you, for God's sake!"

"You brought me here because I was broken!" She was so close she could see tiny droplets of her spittle land on his cheek. "You brought me here so you could be senior detective and finally, finally have it over me!"

"Well, you sure as fuck aren't ready for senior detective, are you?" He sneered. "Are you? Huh? Smashing your laptop, screwing up your own case –"

"And fucking my partner? Go ahead! Go ahead and say it!"

"Going around trying to solve other people's cases! Cases that are closed!"

"What I do on my own time –"

"A girl who's dead a year and a half is none of your fucking business!"

Her mind, steel-trap sharp in her anger, seized on his words. "Crystal Salyers didn't die, she ran away. Isn't that right? Right?"

He gaped, stepped back, his mouth popping open and shut like a fish out of water.

Got you.

"I – I meant," he said, "that she ran away. That's not the… goddamn point, anyway."

She closed the gap between them with one stride. Even now, so close to the end of her rope, her cop mind took over. "How did she die?"

But he had recovered, his righteous indignation back in place. "She ran away."

"That's bullshit. How did she die?"

"She ran away. Her dad died. Case closed, none of your business."

He still wore shirts that were a little too big. She grasped the loose cloth in both fists, yanked him close. "I need to know how she died, and I'm not going to ask you again."

He returned her gesture, grabbing her collar to lock

them in a macabre embrace. "You are not going to do this. You are not going to fuck this up for me. This is my home. This is my life."

"Your life. Your *life*." Her words dripped with contempt. "Stolen lawnmowers. Lost puppies." She let go of his shirt and shoved him backward. "And a suck-ass marriage to a woman you don't love. This is your life. This is what you've done with everything I did for you, with everything *I* gave you."

His eyes suddenly glinted with venom. "Well, at least I didn't kill my partner, now did I?"

The words hit her like a brick. Reality tilted on its axis, twisting into funhouse-mirror shapes as it mocked her. When she said, "You son of a bitch," it was in disbelief more than anything else.

But he wasn't finished. "Maybe you fooled McGann with that bullshit story, but you think you fooled me? There's no way you just quit. No way. You would never have given up on that job. Never. So that means they forced you to quit, and that means they had leverage."

She felt her face begin to quiver. "You... really think that about me. That's what you think of me."

He read her expression as confirmation. "I'm right. Holy shit, I'm right. He'd be alive. He'd be alive right now. Except for you."

She found herself sitting on the rough concrete of the driveway, not sure of how she got there. "Get out of here." Her voice rose into a ragged shout. "Get out. Get out!"

He shone with cruel triumph. "You're taking a vacation day. It's already logged. There's a meeting with the prosecutor at two. If we can't fix this, you're done."

Done. I'm already done.

And then he was gone.

She felt it coming, the muscles of her chest like a steel band around her lungs. She stumbled back to her truck for her purse, fumbled for the pill bottle. She popped one.

And then another.

And then, before she could consider popping the rest of them, she heard the buzzing of her phone.

The screen read, BENSON.

She grabbed the phone, jabbed the answer button with a trembling finger. "Wh-why are you calling me?"

"I saw you called last night. Everything okay?"

She slumped to the ground and sobbed.

Benson asked, "What's wrong?"

"He left me." Her breath came in ragged gasps and the tears poured hot down her face. "He left me."

Andy had prayed for hours, but found no answers. Now, with the clamor of Edna Crowther's television still ringing in her ears, she found herself at the one place where she might find the truth.

She approached the house.

There was crime scene tape stretched across the driveway entrance, so she parked on the road and ducked under it. She felt the bright late-morning heat on her skin. Sweat began to dampen her thin blouse. It was quiet, the only sound the crunch-scuff-pop of her flip-flops as she made her way up the long drive, her shadow flickering beside her. The air was redolent with a smell like hot sap. She remembered the quiet of this place. She tried to let it again surround her and soak into her, but it did not bring the comfort that it once had. As the house loomed closer, she could sense beyond the fading paint and sagging boards that the heart, the soul of the place was gone, drained away and dead. She could just see the outer branches of the oak tree in the back yard. She remembered lying on a blanket under that tree and staring up into the rustling thatch of branches and leaves, sharing truths and secrets with the only real friend she'd ever had, feeling for the first time in her life that the world was a loving world, after all.

Until it wasn't.

She half-expected someone to pop up and yell "Freeze!" like they did on TV, but there was no one. The house was forgotten again. There was more crime scene tape across the door, so she skirted the house, coming around to a side window she knew well. It looked securely latched at first glance, but Crystal had doctored it to provide herself with a way to sneak in and out that her dad wouldn't notice. The innocent-looking five-gallon bucket was still nearby. Andy moved it into place and carefully stepped up onto it, bringing herself even with the window. The window resisted, but finally she cracked the seal of time-fused paint and it yielded, jerking and squawking as it went.

She clambered inside. It was awkward in her skirt, and she scraped her shin painfully on the window frame, losing her balance and tumbling to the floor. Her shoulders and back were still tender from her offering, and stinging pain pushed the breath from her lungs. She clutched her shin, did her best not to curse as her breath returned and the pain subsided. She had to laugh at the absurdity of it, but then she felt the moldy silence of the place and her laughter felt obscene.

The floor was dirty. She swiped at the gray-brown smudge of grime on her skirt. The air felt close, smelling of mildew and smoke. The room was unnaturally cold, her sweat-damp blouse now clammy against her skin.

She breathed in, breathed out.

Crystal. I'm here.

She gazed about the trash-strewn shell that had once been Crystal's living room. Her heart ached with the remembering of things. Watching a "Love Match" marathon in this very room, with the couch pulled right up to the TV because her terrible father had gone to sleep and they had to keep the volume low. Making pancakes in the kitchen that were paper-thin because they'd used too much milk. Letting Crystal give her an awful, clown-face makeover that left them both laughing for hours. Crystal's house was a sanctuary for her, a reprieve from her mother's drugs and whoring, and Crystal's dad did not hurt her when Andy was there. Two people, two hearts, that God had brought together.

Crystal. I'm here.

She moved into the hallway, her footsteps almost reverential, the memories glowing brightly in her mind and cold dread twisting around her heart. She passed the door to the basement. She felt bile rise at the back of her throat.

The voice mail looped in her mind. *"Andy, Andy Please—"*

She reached the foyer.

She turned and faced the house, the stairway leading up, the hallway leading to the now-closed kitchen door. The dusty air tickled her nose and she sneezed. She stood perfectly still, straining to listen, to see if the house would give up its secrets to her. The silence that answered her was unnatural. The dim light and gloomy quiet were reminiscent of a tomb. She breathed in, breathed out, closed her eyes and whispered, "Crystal."

It was a sin to reach out to Crystal in this way, a blasphemy to act as if her dear one's spirit had not moved on as the Bible said all souls did. Eyes still closed, she knelt and felt her knees rest on the old foyer rug, its fibers clotted with filth. "Crystal. Are you here?"

Then she felt it. It was subtle and ethereal at first, a gentle susurration across her mind without words or form. She felt the presence grow in strength, a breeze that seemed solid and aware as it surrounded her, and it electrified her with joy and with terror. She felt warmth return to the air around her. "Crystal," she said in a half-sob, "show me."

She opened her eyes, and gaped in amazement.

The house was as it had been. It was clean, like it had been once before, cleaner than any house she'd ever seen.

The sturdy and boring furniture was back in the living room. The needlepoint Bible verses made by Crystal's aunt hung once again on the walls.

From behind the closed kitchen door, she heard a voice.

Her heart drum-thumping in her chest, Andy rose and moved toward the sound.

Albert Benson, M.D., Ph. D., felt he was coming close to a breakthrough.

His progress with Natasha Briggs was uneven at best. He'd talked her down from a near-suicidal depression after the incident that had left her partner dead and herself badly injured, and counseled her through the anxiety attacks that followed. But once the bigger fires were put out he'd found that his patient had a profound slow-burn of other problems. She was a challenging patient, skillfully parrying his questions, her formidable emotional armor blocking him for over six months. But now, after only a few days after her move to Wright's Crossing, that armor was breaking apart.

It was difficult to maintain his professional detachment as he felt the grief in Natasha's voice. He said, "Tell me why this hurts so much."

"Be-because," she stuttered through her tears, "Because he was su-supposed to back me up. You always ba-back your partner up. Always. Always."

"So you feel betrayed." A sudden thought. "Again."

Her grief detoured into resentment. "I don't know w-why this fucking surprises me. I really d-don't."

"Why do you feel that way?"

"Do you know how many times I kept him from being careless during a traffic stop that turned into a drug bust, kept his ass from getting k-killed? You know how many times I helped him remember procedure so he wouldn't contaminate the evidence chain? Or the time I fudged my testimony so he wouldn't get in trouble for slapping a suspect? I jeopardized my career that time. And he…" Her voice hitched into tears again.

"He left you."

He could hear her voice descend once more into bleak sadness. "He took everything I gave him and he walked away." A moment later, "I guess that's what guys do."

He saw the chance to unlock a subject that she had steadfastly refused to talk about. "Is that what Detective Fletcher did?"

It was a risk to ask that; she could easily shut down on him as she always did when he asked about Fletcher. He held his breath as the seconds seemed to stretch. But then she asked, more to herself than to him it seemed, "Is that what I'm supposed to be sorry for? For Billy?"

"Excuse me?"

She seemed to continue the conversation with herself. "But that doesn't make sense. It doesn't make sense."

"Natasha?"

She exhaled a deep and sorrowful breath. Her voice wavered on the edge of new tears. "You won't believe, you won't fucking believe what I have to tell you about this week."

But then she was silent again. Benson scratched his chin. "Why don't you start by talking about Detec—about Billy? Did he take from you and walk away, like Linc did? Did he leave you too, in his way?"

Her voice replied, almost bewildered, "Billy? No. He didn't do that." Another pause. "At least, not in the same way."

"How do you mean?"

"I mean, working with Billy was different."

"How?"

Silence again. Then, "Billy was ambitious. He was smart. He… he understood."

"What did he understand? That there's more to life

than stolen lawnmowers?"

She sighed in irritation, but her voice had softened when she finally responded. "Billy wanted to get ahead, he wasn't afraid to push it. I mean, the two years we worked together we had the highest closing ratio in the department, and we were the youngest detectives there."

"So I guess you two were well-matched."

"Maybe that was the problem."

"Problem?" Benson listened, strained to hear any change in her breathing, her tone, the only indicators he had for what she might be feeling.

She asked, "You want to know what happened that night he and I went into that house? What really happened?"

His fingers froze in his beard mid-scratch. "Of course."

"Most of it... Most of it is the same as what I told you, what I told everyone. We were staking out that house on crack row 'cause we heard that Reg Montblanc's new girlfriend stayed there sometimes."

"You couldn't go in, correct?"

"Right, we couldn't get a warrant. Only way to go in was if we saw him through the window or through the door. So we couldn't go in. And we were really pissed."

"Why?"

"'Cause we knew he was there. We *knew* it. The motherfucker beat his ex-wife to death with their son's baseball bat, and he was just sitting in there waiting for us to leave or fall asleep or get called away."

"But then you did see him, through the window, correct?"

Her voice cracked. "No. We didn't."

"Go on."

"We figured we'd say that we saw him look out the window, that he looked like he had made us for cops so we had to go in right then. He'd deny it, but who was gonna believe him, right? So we went in, didn't wait for backup, kicked in the front door like a… TV show."

Benson listened.

"There was a hallway. There was a woman screaming somewhere. It was an old house. The kitchen was the room farthest back. I ended up in front of Billy somehow. I went into the kitchen and…" Her voice became weighted with sorrow as she confronted the memory. "I thought… I thought Billy was right behind me. Montblanc was there, in the kitchen, he got the jump on me. He had a length of pipe. He beat me bad." Her voice faded to almost nothing. "Really bad."

Benson listened.

"I told Billy to stick close when we went in. With just two of us, there was no other way to do it."

"But he didn't."

"Billy… Billy was a rock star. Soon as you turned your back, he'd start doing his own thing. Just like me."

Benson discovered he was holding his breath.

"So, I'm bleeding and bashed up and I'm dragging myself across the kitchen floor with the one arm that still works. Montblanc's standing there, he's got my gun. He's had his fun breaking my bones and watching me bleed, so now he's going to kill me, and I'm staring down the barrel of my own gun, and that's when Billy shows up."

"And he shot Montblanc."

"He panicked. And Montblanc panicked. And they just started shooting. You call it a 'spray and pray.' Sometimes, you know, people are five feet away from each other and they shoot until their guns are empty and no one lands a shot."

"What happened this time?"

She inhaled, paused, exhaled. "Montblanc got hit three times. He made it out of the kitchen, but he collapsed in the hallway. Billy fell where he stood. I looked into his face, you know that? I saw the life go out of his eyes."

"I'm sorry."

"Linc thinks they forced me out, but he's wrong. My career was fucked, yeah. They would have kicked me down to burglary or missing persons, or maybe even back to patrol. But I never got that far. First day back at work, I took three steps through the door and had a panic attack, had to go to the hospital 'cause I couldn't breathe. You... well, you know the rest."

Benson did.

"I've been having this nightmare ever since I got out of the hospital. It's me, back on that kitchen floor, and I can see the blood, there's blood all over, and the floor smells like bacon grease, and Montblanc is standing over me. And I'm scared."

Benson could feel it coming. "Why exactly are you scared, in that moment?"

"Because I'm going to die. He's going to kill me. And... there's nothing I can do about it. *Nothing*."

Something about this dream was significant, he could feel it. "What is his face like? What is his expression? Is he angry? Happy?"

"He's..." She stopped. A note of confusion entered her voice. "I don't know."

"Why not?"

"Because I never... I never actually see his face." That fact seemed to have a profound meaning for her. "That floor," she said. "That kitchen floor."

"What about it?"

In a snap, the conversation dead-ended. "It... had rat turds on it. That's all." She had closed herself to him again, but he sensed that something had changed, a revelation that she had uncovered but would not share. "Thank you, Doctor Benson. I really appreciate you calling."

"You said a minute ago you had something to tell me. About this week."

But he already knew the conversation was over. "It was nothing. I'll call you next week." And with that, he heard the *beep* of the call ending.

Benson had a fleeting, inexplicable feeling that this would be the last time he would ever talk to Natasha Briggs. But there was a mound of paperwork to deal with before his first appointment of the day, and the feeling was quickly forgotten.

Andy lay fetal on the floor of Crystal's house. The house was dirty and cold and burnt and dead, as it had been.

She sobbed, "I'm sorry, Crystal. I'm sorry. I'm sorry."

Natasha hit the "end call" button, and lay back on the couch.

Well, Benson, I guess I owe you one.

She rose stiffly and moved to the kitchen to put some coffee on. She realized she was thirsty, poured herself a glass of water from the tap and guzzled it, then another. There was peanut butter, but no bread, so she slathered it onto crackers and snarfed. Sipping coffee after her feast, roaming the tiny kitchen space with her tired eyes, she almost laughed at the irony of it all.

All the times she'd had that nightmare, she'd never made the connection about the kitchen.

Montblanc's kitchen had not smelled of bacon grease, but of rat poison. And it hadn't been dirty, either; the faded linoleum on that floor was clean enough to eat off of. The filthy kitchen floor that had smelled like bacon grease had been her own, the kitchen of the shithole trailer in Martinsville, the floor her mother died on. She remembered sitting on that horrible floor, bawling, helpless as the blood (so much blood) poured from the wound in her unconscious mother's head, the blood reaching for her, soaking into her jeans, staining the skin of her bare feet, while Daddy babbled on the phone to the 911 operator.

She always woke up from the nightmare before the gun went off, because there was no gun. The kitchen in the dream was her own. And the monster in the dream was her own.

Girl, you'll never get away from this place.

That was what her father said to her, that night at the Gas-N-Go. It had puzzled her, the way he said it. It was never his style to be that straightforward. He was an expert at the kind of smooth, surgical insult that could break the neck of your hopes and dreams with one subtle twist. His whole useless, shitty life, he'd used his words and his fists to keep those closest to him as low-down as he. It was only now Natasha realized that, in his way, her father had for once tried to give her some heartfelt advice.

You were right, Daddy. I never got away from that place, because I never got away from you. As far as I got, as hard as I ran, I never got clear of you. And here I was, about to spill it to Benson, to just lay down and give up, just like you always wanted.

Her body quietly begged for more sleep. Instead, she grabbed her phone.

I won't give up, Daddy. Not while I've still got a chance.

She dialed a number and listened to it ring.

Are you sorry. That's what she said. Sinners must burn.

But sorry for what? For Billy? No, Billy would have gone in alone if she hadn't been there. For Montblanc? Definitely not. So what was it?

There was another possibility, of course. She hadn't told Benson everything about that night. Some secrets were still hers to keep. But when she compared herself to what she knew of Grace Randolph, their lives and their respective sins did not line up.

Grace. What did you do? What did I do? Are we even guilty of the same crime?

She had precious little time, but her best chance, it seemed, lay with Grace. If she could uncover the crime for which the ghost had judged Grace, perhaps she could find a way to survive.

The ghost will come again tonight.

She knew without knowing how that she would not survive another attack from the creature that had once been Crystal Salyers.

Today was her last chance.

Andy marched into her apartment. Her eyes glittered with righteous wrath.

She flung open the door of her closet sanctuary, absently tossing her purse in the corner. She yanked at her blouse, almost savoring the sound as the worn fabric tore. She imagined herself standing naked before the congregation of her church, ready to receive their judgement and punishment, her sins painted on her body in blood.

God had said, "Those whom I love, I reprove and discipline, so be zealous and repent." It was from Revelations, one of her favorite verses.

She pulled off her bra and slammed the closet door shut.

She knelt and whipped the chain furiously against her back, again and again and again.

"Murderer!" punctuated each and every blow. "MURDERER!"

She continued until she blacked out from the pain.

Natasha sipped coffee as Merriman dropped a folder marked "Randolph, Grace" in front of her. The thinness of the file was not encouraging. She asked, "This is everything?"

"It's weird that there's a clipping file for her at all. Old Rickman, the guy who owned this paper before it went under? People say he got kind of senile toward the end and did these clipping files himself, just locked himself in his office and clipped articles all day and half the night. One of these days I'll get them all in the database, but…" He trailed off, must have noticed she wasn't paying attention to him.

The articles were a disappointment. "Students honored by Mayor." "French Club Officers Named." "ECHS Volleyball Wins Regionals."

Merriman watched her appraisingly from the other side of his desk. He had not yet touched his own coffee. "Find what you needed?"

She sat back and rubbed her eyes. She replied "No," and realized too late the mistake of telling him anything. *Fuck*. It had made sense for her to start here, with the low-hanging fruit, but the time was already pushing noon and she was nowhere.

Merriman's look was odd. "I don't suppose you could tell me what it is you're looking for?"

"Not without sounding nuts."

His reply surprised her. "You wouldn't be the first."

She looked up, her eyes narrowing. "Explain."

He leaned back in his chair, finally picked up his coffee and swigged. "They say the first white person to set foot in this county was a witch, you know that?"

"No."

He smiled. "Not something they advertise. Her name was Mary Wright. Got convicted of witchcraft and 'conspiring with the Lord of Evil' in Jamestown in 1624. She seduced the jailer, cut his throat, and escaped. She crossed the river here trying to get away, but a preacher named Colvin and his gang tracked her down. Word is they burned her at the stake. Named the town after her and the county after him."

She remembered something from a high school history book. "No one got burned at the stake in this country. That only happened in Europe."

"So they say."

I don't have time for this. "Your point is?"

He leaned forward. "This is also the county where a local slave owner and his family were found dead in their beds, with their eyes removed so cleanly there wasn't a spot of blood on the sheets. There's a cave near the village of Colvin where over the years five unmarried couples have been found dead, with no sign of what killed them and their bodies not decayed until they were removed from the cave. There's a lake where one of the nation's first serial killers drowned kids for fun, and since then no fish or any other animal life can live in it." A surprisingly delicate finger tapped the desk blotter in cadence to his voice, which had become hushed, tense. "I could go on. The point is, there's more stories like that in this county that anywhere in the state. I've looked. So no, I wouldn't think you're nuts." His hand smoothed a non-existent wrinkle from his shirt. "And if you don't mind me saying, you do owe me one."

She was seeing a different part of Chad Merriman, but what part that was she could not determine. It was almost 12:30, and there was nothing more he could do to help her. She pushed back the childish urge to confide, to confess. "Tell you what, Merriman. Keep the police scanner on tonight, starting at nine."

His eyebrows rose. "What's going to happen?"

She rose. "Not sure, but it's going to be something big."

She had taken to driving the side streets as much as she could, feeling a growing paranoia take hold that McGann was watching her, that he had sent an informal BOLO on her to the day officers. She remembered another snippet of history book trivia, a quote from some Civil War soldier, *there is nothing so much like God on Earth as a general on the battlefield.* Or a small-town police chief.

She was now parked in a weedy lot behind a church

that was boarded up and closed. The faded sign still blared, "Barbecue Tonite! We can save our church!" She worked to ignore the growling in her stomach while she waited. Her phone was on speaker, and she could hear the faint sound of keys tapping. Then the voice came back on. "Okay, I think I'm in."

"You're incredible, Randall."

"You just love me for my body."

"What can you see?"

She heard another few taps, a strident BEEP. "Nothing."

"She's clean?"

"Like the new-fallen snow."

She glanced at the dashboard clock. It read: 1:07.

"I assume we're talking about her juvenile record?"

"That'd be sealed."

She snapped, "Jesus, Randall, the girl was sixteen! Why do I need a goddamn adult criminal record search for a sixteen-year-old girl?" She caught herself, too late. *Bad move, bad bad move.* She took a breath, forced her tone to lighten. "I'm... I'm sorry. I'm sorry, Randall. I'm... having a rough day."

There was a taut silence. Then Randall exhaled an "Okay." A moment later, "I know I can't get in there, but maybe I can see if there is a juvenile record at all." Tapping of keys, BEEP. "Nothing. Miss Randolph's got nothing to be ashamed of, or at least nothing she got caught for."

Or nothing her money couldn't buy her out of. She had nothing. The day was over half gone and she had nothing.

"Detective?"

She managed a "Thank you, Randall," and pushed "end" without waiting to hear his reply. This call would get back to McGann, somehow. Everything did.

Wait a second...

Something was working its way to the front of her mind. The argument with Linc. He'd accused her of talking to Eddie Shifflett without his lawyer, but he'd said nothing about the incident at the church last night, which had to mean he didn't know.

Andy didn't tell. Why not?

She remembered the sight of Andy in the parking lot, her face bitter with rage – "You fucking cops. You fucking cops!" – and yet she hadn't complained to the police. More importantly, she likely hadn't told anyone in her church, either. Someone would have called on her behalf, even if she asked them not to. The chance to score some points against the police was just too good to pass up.

It wasn't much, but it told Natasha enough. She said a silent prayer of gratitude for her habit of always putting important numbers in her phone while she was working a case. She dialed Andy's cell number, but got voice mail. Not bothering to leave a message, she started the truck. The back tires spun on the crumbling asphalt before finding purchase. The car jumped forward as it sped away from the church, and Natasha hung on.

Andy's address was a sad old Victorian that had long ago been carved into apartments. A skeletal old black man held sentry duty on the sagging front porch. He nodded at Natasha as she approached, an evil-smelling cigar smoldering in one hand. "Help you?"

"Andy Wagner."

He seemed to savor the time it took him to consider her request. The front yard of the house was littered with faded plastic toys and smelled of dog shit. "That'd be the girl in number four, round the back." She could feel his questioning eyes on her back as she walked around the side of the house. The sun beat down fiercely on her neck.

The enterprising landlord had dug out room for a small staircase and a door for a basement apartment. The concrete that lined each side of the descent was cracked and warped. The sun did not reach this space, and she savored the clammy coolness. The doorbell button had been broken off. She knocked and was startled by how the flimsy door shook with the impact, the sound echoing about the confines of the small space. There was no answer. She knocked until her knuckles were red.

Her watch read: 1:52. She would miss the meeting with the prosecutor.

Suddenly, from above, "You come 'bout the dog?"

She jerked around, hand reflexively going to her gun, but all that stood at the top of the stairs was the old black man. He still held his cigar; the stink made her guts tighten. "Excuse me?"

"You the police, right? I been callin' about the dog next door."

She breathed *in on four, out on eight*, trying to keep her chest from spasming. "I'm not here about the dog."

He frowned. "Can't get nobody to come out. Dog's barkin' all night and shittin' in the yard, you know?"

She breathed deep to keep from snapping like she had with Randall. "Do you know Miss Wagner? Do you have any idea where she is?"

"'Fraid not. Don't know her too well."

"Is her car parked on the street?"

"Don't see it, but most times we all gotta park way down the block, 'cause all the houses on this street are apartments and there's too many cars. You want to look inside? I got the key."

"Are you the owner?"

"Kinda the manager."

She almost gave up, almost dashed back to her truck to haul ass to the meeting with the prosecutor, fall on her sword and beg for forgiveness, spend her last day on earth as a cop and wait patiently for the horrors of the night. Then she replied, "Fine. I would like to look inside."

The apartment was small, a kitchen area with ratty table and chairs to one side, a bed on the opposite side, a closet and tiny bathroom built out from the far wall. There was no couch or television. The place was neat as a pin but spartan and dreary, a perfect reflection of its tenant. The bathroom door was open, but no one was inside.

Natasha made a cursory inspection of the place. There was no sign of Andy – or her purse or cell phone. *Goddamn it. Goddamn it.* She fought to keep from shouting in frustration.

The old man asked, "So what she done?"

"I just need to talk to her. Do you know where she spends her time?"

"She don't neighbor much."

I don't have time. The words began to chatter rhythmically in her ear. *I don't have time. I don't have time.* She brushed past him, bracing herself against the stifling heat and unrelenting sun as she mounted the stairs. She turned and said, "Thank you for your help," and was off again.

"You gonna do something about that dog?"

"We'll be in touch."

Back in the truck, she suddenly realized she hadn't checked inside the closet. *Shit. Shit!* She was tired, getting frantic, making mistakes left and right, now. For a moment she thought about going back, but decided against it. There'd been no sign of Andy's purse or cell phone. Andy Wagner didn't strike her as the type to hide from the cops in the closet.

The air conditioning needed to get up to speed after the time she'd spent away from the truck; the blast of damp, half-cool air that it pushed into her face made her think of the earthy confines of the grave.

There was a voice mail and a text from Linc. She ignored them.

The dashboard clock read: 2:10. There was another

card she could play, but it was one that carried serious repercussions if it went wrong. She'd need to play it now or never.

I don't have time. I don't have time.

She made her decision. Instead of turning left at the next intersection toward the church, she turned right, toward the school.

The principal of Colvin High School said, "I'm not sure I'm comfortable with this, Officer." He was short and balding and sported a prominent brown stain on a shirt that had seen too many washings. They sat in a dim, airless conference room. Outside the open door, an elderly secretary cast sideways glances at them.

Natasha replied, in her best professional-cop voice, "It's just some routine follow-up. I appreciate your help." She tried to remember his name.

He hesitated, made a "Hmmmmuha" sound as he deliberated, but the arrival of the two girls seemed to decide the issue. He stood – a real gentleman, this guy – and said, "Girls, I think you know Detective Briggs?"

Caitlin stood with a hand on one hip and a leg subtly bouncing, while Hanna, as usual, drooped behind her. Neither said a word.

Natasha said, "Please close the door and sit down."

They took a seat with a sullen wariness that was normal for two teens called to the principal's office. The clock on the wall was the old-fashioned kind, the synchronized school clock system where the minute hand moved forward with an audible CLICK. The sound had already become like a pinprick in Natasha's mind.

For the principal more than anything else, she started with, "I appreciate this, girls. I'm sure this is a difficult time for you."

They replied with the same mumble-nod combination she remembered from their last meeting.

CLICK.

I don't have time. I don't have time.

"I need to know something, and it's important. I'm convinced that Grace did something, sometime before she died. It was something bad, something she was... sorry for. I need to know what she did. It's important." She could sense the principal shifting in his seat beside her. He felt the interview turning serious, and she needed to be careful.

The girls exchanged a puzzled look. Caitlin asked, "Something bad? Like what?"

CLICK. Natasha felt the hand around her pen begin to curl into a fist.

"That's what I'm asking. Did she tell you about something she did, something she regretted?"

Caitlin shrugged. "She smoked weed, she cut school, she stole money from her mom, I don't know."

Hanna suddenly piped up with, "She slept with my boyfriend."

Caitlin rolled her eyes. "She wasn't sorry for that."

CLICK.

"Girls," Natasha replied, feeling the edge in her voice and unable to smooth it, "I don't have time for this. I need you to think."

Caitlin said, "Think what? Like, did she kill somebody? I don't know."

Natasha felt her breathing quicken, fought to stay controlled. "Just tell me what she did. Grace died because of something she did and I need to know what it was and I'm running out of time."

CLICK.

She could feel the principal tensing, saw the change in Caitlin's face as the teenage attitude came out. "Running out of time? She's fucking dead already."

The principal said, "Caitlin, that's not appropriate language."

"Well she's, like, going off on me."

Natasha said, "Just tell me what she did." The principal's frown was a warning bell that she found herself unable to heed. "You're not in trouble. But I need to know what it was. Now."

Hanna interjected, "Should we get a lawyer or something?"

CLICK.

Natasha slammed her fist on the table. "What was she sorry for?!" All three of them jumped back in unison. "Goddamn it, what was she sorry for?!"

Shocked silence.

It was Hanna who spoke next. "Grace wasn't sorry for anything. She was too rich to be sorry."

Then, Mister Principal. "This meeting is over."

CLICK.

The time was 3:34 as she sped out of the school parking lot. The principal would call and complain. She'd be fired for sure, now, possibly even arrested, but her job was the least of her worries right now.

One hand on the wheel, she dialed Andy's number again, and again got no answer. "Andy," she said, as the voice mail kicked in, "this is Detective Briggs. I'm... I'm very sorry about last night, but I need you to call me as soon as possible. I need your help. And I think you're the only one who can help me. Please call me."

I need your help. It made her half-crazy to need someone's help, let alone ask for it.

She accelerated. The school receded in the rearview mirror.

Linc was sitting in a church so he wouldn't get drunk. He didn't know what else to do.

I blew. I blew it. God damn me, I blew it again.

It was a Catholic church. He was only here because it

was the first church he'd come to, but it turned out he'd chosen well. It was built in the old style, high-ceilinged, ornate fretwork, stained glass windows on each side. The room seemed to absorb sound and amplify the distance between him and the scattering of old folks who were the nave's only other occupants. It made him feel alone, which was how he wanted to feel.

Of course you blew it. That's all you ever did.

His phone warbled. It was McGann. He ignored it. After Nat hadn't shown up for the meeting, he'd told the desk officer he was going to look for her, ignoring the little bastard's smirk as he turned away.

There was only one time in your life you didn't blow it. When you were with her.

As he turned off his phone, the time read: 4:17.

Nat. Oh, Nat.

A phone call to the church had provided Natasha with an address, the home of a parishioner that Andy had set out to visit that morning and not returned from.

The name on the battered, rusting mailbox read, "Crowther." Natasha's heart sank as she saw no other car on the overgrown strip of gravel that made up the driveway. She got out anyway; the time was 4:46 and she was running out of options. The house was a singlewide trailer as worn as the mailbox. She knocked and almost instantly heard a strident, "Come in!" from inside. She had no sooner stepped a foot into the house when the voice followed up with, "Hurry up! I ain't cooling the whole outside!" She hustled the rest of the way in, doing an awkward mambo with the door as she tried to close it quickly.

The living room that the front door opened into was a jumble of outdated furnishings, carpeting, and wallpaper, but it was clean enough. A massively obese old woman, her legs swathed in bandages, rested in a recliner to the left. A TV blared. The old woman's bitter expression darkened further when she beheld Natasha. "Who the hell are you?"

"I'm... looking for Andy Wagner. Was she here?"

The old woman went back to glowering at the mention of Andy's name. "She was here. High-tailed it out of here fast enough."

"Do you know where she went? Do you have any idea where she is?"

"Ain't my job to watch her." She turned back to the TV. "Girl's got her head up her ass."

Natasha hesitated, unable to think of something, anything she could ask the woman to help her in her search, losing her words and furious with herself for it. *I don't have time. I don't have time.*

The old woman turned her dagger-eyed glare back to Natasha. It seemed to puzzle her that Natasha was still there. She squinted. "You don't do much prayin', do you?"

Caught off guard, Natasha could only mumble, "I...why do you ask?"

"Didn't think so. That's why you're here, you know."

"I, I don't understand."

The old woman suddenly smiled, a nasty smile, but there was a dark wisdom in her eyes that Natasha could not ignore. "Don't do no prayin', bet you ain't been to church in Lord knows how long. See it in your eyes. You got troubles, got the devil after you, no doubt. Ain't no surprise to me." She turned back to the TV by way of dismissal. "Wherever you're running, won't be far enough." And with that, she was silent.

Natasha hustled out the door, stripped bare by the woman's judgement.

She felt herself coming undone, felt that she might start crying, and if she did she knew she wouldn't be able to stop. She fumbled one-handed in the glove compartment for a granola bar. There was one left, and somehow the simple joy of that made her want to start crying again.

I don't have time. I don't have time.

The truck sprayed gravel as she shot back toward town.

Andy staggered out the door of her apartment. Her head throbbed. Her back was a rippling mass of pain and she whimpered and jerked with each step. At first she did not believe the time of 6:41 that shone from her watch, but the waning sun and the softening heat were proof enough. She could feel the heavy air coalesce around her, trying to hinder her, making her pain all the worse. But she did not waver. Her self-punishment had brought her back to herself, but it had not cleansed her. Not nearly. She needed to find Detective Briggs.

She rounded the side of the building to find Tucker on his porch, engaged in his usual evening routine of alternating puffs on his cigar with sips of a tallboy beer. "Miz Wagner," he said.

"Evening, Tucker."

"Didn't see you come back. Po-lice was lookin' for you."

She could feel her voice distend with suppressed pain. "Okay. Thank you."

She did her best to walk normally, but she must have failed because the next thing she heard was, "You alright, there?"

She turned her head and winced with the pain of it. "Fine. Headache. I'll see you later."

He nodded in that somber way of his, as if they had just shared a deep truth between them. The reek of his cigar ratcheted up the ache in her head and she thought she might faint.

As she turned left down the sidewalk, dreading the two-block trek to her car, Tucker called out, "So what you done?"

She gingerly pivoted on her heel in order to face him. "We're all guilty of something, ain't we?" Then she turned and continued her pain-shuffle down the sidewalk.

When she finally reached her car, she ruffled through her purse for her cell phone and realized the battery was dead and the charger back in her apartment.

Natasha sat in her truck, now parked across from the Randolph house, as the translucent light of summer evening crept about her.

She had gone from the old woman's house back to Andy's apartment, from the apartment to the church. She'd left message after message for Andy with no response. Now she waited, sick with frustration and fear, to play the one card she had left. There was only one other person who could enlighten her about the sin that Grace had died for, and that person was currently not home.

Her truck stuck out in this neighborhood like a sore thumb. She'd already been accosted by two concerned citizens, told them the same lie about possible threats against the Randolph family. The lie wouldn't hold for long.

I don't have time. I don't have time. The mantra had gained force as the hours ticked away. It boomed and sniggered and mocked her. *I don't have time. I don't have time. What did Grace do? What did she do?*

It wasn't dying that she feared, but the pain, the fear, the madness of it. She knew deep down that it was too late to prevent the coming attack, even if by some miracle she could convince Denise Randolph to admit to her daughter's transgressions, but she had set herself on this track as her one and only hope, and there was nothing else to do but follow it to the end. Her stomach ached. The granola bar had not been nearly enough to soak up the acid of her growing panic. She licked the sticky residue from inside a coffee cup. Her vision blurred as she fought her weariness and hunger to stay alert.

When her vision cleared, the dashboard clock read: 8:01, and Denise Randolph's Mercedes had appeared like magic in the driveway.

Almost instantly, she was across the street, her finger hammering on the doorbell button. Her fatigue vanished as the chance for salvation and survival surged through her once again. She heard footsteps approach the door, hesitate. *They're looking through the peephole.* Then, a low murmur of voices. Silence. The door opened and a stone-faced Maria appeared. "Mrs. Randolph is not home."

Oh, no you don't.

"That's her car in the driveway, isn't it?"

"She...is letting me use it. She took her other car."

Natasha leaned in and said, in a quiet voice, "Maria?"

Reflexively, the housekeeper leaned in as well. "Yes?"

"Denise Randolph wouldn't let you drive her Mercedes to save her fucking life." And with one smooth movement, she placed her palm against Maria's breastbone and shoved.

Natasha marched down the hallway, ignoring Maria's angry cries as the housekeeper struggled back to her feet. The air conditioning in the house was on full-blast and her sweat-soaked clothing instantly clung to her. She stormed into the living room to find Denise, her stance the very picture of haughty defiance. Denise hissed, "I will have your job for this. I will have your *job.*"

Natasha didn't break stride, brought herself up to within two feet of the other woman. Denise had made the error of standing too close to the side of the couch. It prevented her from backing up, and her glower wrinkled with discomfort as she found her personal space invaded. "My job," Natasha growled, "is the least of my worries, Mrs. Randolph. Grace did something, something bad, something she was sorry for. It's the reason she died, and you know what it is. And you're going to tell me."

But Denise did not break. Her eyes went black and her mouth spread into a rictus of malice. "Didn't you hear the news? Grace killed herself. She burned herself alive. Isn't that enough? Isn't that enough for you?"

Natasha felt the room shrink, felt a bolt of white-hot fury rise up in her at the creature before her that dared call itself a mother. "Is it enough for *you*? Was it punishment enough for whatever she did, whatever it was that cut your vacation short?" She brought her face inches from Denise's. "You didn't even realize she was gone until we called, did you? You didn't even *notice*."

"You," Denise replied, her voice coarse with hatred and her breath saturated with alcohol, "can go straight to hell for all I care."

The next moment, the gun was in Natasha's trembling hand, inches from Denise's forehead, and the woman's contempt instantly drained to shock. Natasha heard her own voice, tinged with madness, reply, "You first."

Pain exploded against the back of her head. She staggered under its force, felt another blow slam into her temple. *Maria.*

She felt the floor rise up to meet her, fell to her knees and fought to keep the room from spinning. There was blood trickling down the side of her head, the shattered remnants of an earthenware lamp scattered about the floor, and the sound of a revved engine, screeching tires outside.

She struggled to get back on her feet. *Come back. Tell me. Tell me.*

But the floor shifted again, and the room blurred and melted into darkness.

Natasha regained her senses and knew her time was

9:13

up.

The house was empty and quiet, a dead place. As she stumbled down the hall toward the door, her head blaring with pain, it seemed like she was actually dreaming of walking through this house, reality and unreality flickering back and forth at the whim of some force outside herself. The front door gaped open. The outside air settled on her like a damp blanket. She reached her truck, leaning against the grill and breathing deep.

Her watch read: 9:10.

She laughed. She didn't know what else to do.

9:11.

She discovered that her gun was still clutched in her right hand. For a moment, she contemplated using it.

9:12.

She holstered the gun and pushed off of the truck, steadying herself. She slowed her breathing and stared into the night.

"At least this time," she said, "I'm going to look you in the eye."

9:13.

And then, nothing.

Nothing happened. No ghost. No pain. Nothing.

9:14.

9:15.

She felt a dangerous kind of laughter well up inside of her, clamped down on it, standing ready.

At 9:20, she let herself breathe.

She rested her back against the grill of the truck, looked into the night sky. "I'm crazy," she said. "I'm crazy, I'm fired, I'm going to jail."

And it's okay. Crazy is okay.

And then her phone tittered.

The screen read: LINC.

She hit the "answer" button, pressed the phone to

her ear. "Babe," she said, her voice high and bright and halfway to a giggle, "After you arrest me, I've got some shit to tell you that —"

"Nat?" It took her a moment to recognize the hoarse, terrified voice was Linc's. "Are you there, Nat? Are you there?"

Her euphoria evaporated and alarm took its place. "Linc? What is it? Where are you?" She was already in her truck, gunning the engine, starting a U-turn.

"Home. I'm at home. Nat, please. Please —"

"I'm on my way. I'm on my way." She spun the wheel with one hand to turn, cursed the ant-farm layout of the neighborhood's streets as she concentrated on finding the way out. "Linc, what is it? What is —" The call cut off. She hammered the redial as she shot past the guard house and onto the main road, but it went to voice mail. "Shit. Shit!"

She knew then that she was not crazy. A terrible fear began to spread through her, frigid and sharp under her skin. Finally reaching the main road, she hammered the accelerator and shot toward Linc's neighborhood.

There were no lights on in Linc's house.

The street was deserted as she veered into the driveway, the quiet unnatural as she jumped from the truck. She licked her dust-dry lips and shivered.

She noticed a light peeking through the tiny gap around the garage door. From inside the garage, there were sounds — muttering, weeping.

Praying.

Her heart thumping in a rapid staccato, she reached into Linc's still-unlocked car and pressed the garage door opener with a trembling hand. The door squealed this time as it opened, perhaps because of the humid air, and the sound scraped against her nerves.

One hand on her gun, she approached.

9:13

Shapes and forms came into focus slowly as the door revealed the garage's contents. A single bare bulb cast weird shadows that made the complete picture indistinct. But Linc, standing oddly straight in the middle of the space, was clear enough, and at the sight of his pallid skin and ghastly expression her lungs felt drained of breath. Before she could speak, before she could put another foot in front of the other, he said, "Don't. Stay where you are."

She stopped, stricken. "Linc, Goddamn it, what –"

"What did you see? What did you see, the night I was at your house?"

She gawked at him, the truth behind his question leaving her slack-jawed, horror blossoming ever deeper inside her. "I... I saw a chain. Around your neck." She found another breath and asked, "What did you see?"

His face contorted in grief. "I saw you. On fire."

Oh my God. Oh my God.

She could not move, the enormity of it robbing her limbs of their motion. "You... you saw her. You've seen. You've been haunted. Oh, Jesus, she... Linc, tell me. Tell me."

But in reply he asked, "You remember the day I sent you that email, about how we had an opening for detective?"

She nodded. "I remember."

"You know it was my anniversary the day I emailed you?" The light bulb flickered. His skin seemed to glisten in the strange, shadowy glow.

"Linc." She took a step closer. "Baby, I –"

"You can't come closer!" She stopped. *Something's wrong. Something's wrong.*

"Linc, you can talk to me, you can... tell me."

His face quivered. "I was sitting, I was s-sitting in that car with flowers and candy and some cheapshit bracelet I bought, and I couldn't go home. I couldn't go home." He bowed his head and wept. His body shook, but he made no attempt to wipe his eyes. He looked up again. "You know why I left you, Nat? I couldn't match you. I couldn't even keep up with you, and it pissed me off. That's it. That's all it was. But if I'd been with you that night, if I'd gone into that house with you, I would have been right behind you. All the way, I'd have been right behind you."

She felt her own tears spilling down her cheeks. "I know. I know that. I know."

"I'm sorry," he said. "I'm sorry."

It was then she noticed the smell. Pungent and chemical and strong. Her face clouded with confusion and fear. "Linc, what —"

Gasoline!

He wailed, "I knew she didn't run away! I knew it! And I didn't do anything!"

Oh, no. Oh sweet Jesus, NO!

But he had already raised the lighter. "Sinners must burn."

The garage erupted in a WHUMP! Fire obliterated him from her sight. For a moment, her shrieks matched his.

And the next moment, the horrible specter of Crystal Salyers emerged from the flames. Its skin glowed hideous shades of orange-gray in the refraction of the firelight, its face a shimmering mask of hatred.

Natasha's courage dissolved, panic knocked her legs into backward motion toward her car. The ghost advanced amid the pops and whooshes of other flammables igniting, the garage already an inferno. Natasha shoved the keys into the ignition, jolted against her seat as she slammed the truck into reverse. Tires squealed as the specter receded in the windshield's view.

She realized she was still screaming.

She shoved the gearshift into D and the truck barreled down the street.

9:13

She careened through an intersection, around a corner, one street melding into another, moving by instinct and reflex, an animal in threat and unmindful of anything but flight.

Then the adrenaline-numbness in her mind receded slightly, and she realized she was back at her house, her truck idling at the foot of the driveway, facing the garage.

And Crystal Salyers stood before her.

She'd never had the chance to look at the ghost closely, see its filthy, emaciated frame, the sturdy chain around its neck, its glare of malevolent evil. It stood in front of the closed garage door, for all the world an earthly being, blocking her path. And then it smiled.

It was a ghastly smile, a grimace of gleeful spite, and it broke through the cloud of fear and sorrow that sought to paralyze Natasha, transformed it into the raw rage of survival.

Natasha roared.

She stomped the accelerator. The truck's tires screamed against the concrete, the stench of burned rubber stinging her nostrils, the truck rocketing forward at the leering specter. The truck smashed through the garage door, slammed against the inside wall with a wrenching impact, and Natasha heard the world go quiet as the airbag lashed her face.

It might have been seconds or minutes before she tumbled out of the truck, felt the coolness of the concrete against her stinging cheek. She struggled to ground herself and realign her reeling senses as she wobbled to her feet.
She faced the empty garage, her breaths ragged and deep. "I," she growled, "am not… sorry." Then, louder. "I'm not sorry. I AM NOT SORRY!"

An incredible pain erupted in her abdomen.

She gasped, but the pain was a vise that clamped her lungs closed. She fell to the floor, flat on her back, immobilized in her agony. The pain seemed to burn, to writhe like a living thing, hell itself burning inside her and struggling to tear its way out. She opened her mouth to scream, but all she managed was a strangled, choking sound.

Her belly began to swell.

She could only watch in torment as it grew, stretching two feet, four feet, long past all natural size, as something beneath the skin, something horrible and alive, rippled and twisted.

A tiny point of red appeared at the top of the grotesque distention. Blood. A tearing, ripping.

A full-sized human hand, then an arm, slithered out of the bloody wound.

Natasha found her scream.

Another hand appeared, tearing the hole wider, wider. Blood, so much blood, as a head appeared, a face.

Crystal.

The thing that had been Crystal Salyers climbed from the gory ruin of Natasha's body, naked and bloody and dripping with a black, sulfurous slime, as Natasha gurgled in madness from the pain and horror.

The thing stood over her and said, "You will be."

Natasha uttered her final scream as her body burst into flames and the ghost of Crystal Salyers howled in triumph.

It was only a few moments later that Natasha came back to herself, her body intact and her mind in pieces.

She found the strength to stand. Her limbs were flaccid, resistant to her commands, but she pushed them onward. There was no question of what she would do.

She staggered to the steaming wreck of her truck, found her purse, and fumbled in it for her pill bottle. She lurched through the garage door into the house. Inside, she flopped to the floor of the kitchen, opened a nearby cupboard, and pulled out the jar of moonshine that Linc had given her.

9:13

It took a few minutes for her weak and shaking hands to pop the top on the pill bottle, to twist off the recalcitrant lid of the mason jar.

She swallowed the pills. Every last one.

She drank the moonshine. Every last drop.

The floor rose gently to meet her. Her cheek resting on the linoleum, her sidelong view of the kitchen began to shrink, as if she was seeing it at the end of a tunnel that got longer and longer.

She closed her eyes.

Time's a-wasting, and for the first time in her career, Natasha is balking.

Billy, polished and brilliant and unstoppable, says, "Tasha, we've got to go in."

She hates how he calls her Tasha, but won't let him call her Nat. She swallows, utterly unfamiliar with this feeling of caution. "Maybe," she stammers, "maybe we should wait. For backup. He's —"

Billy groans like a schoolboy kept in from recess. "Tasha, for Christ's sake." She can see it drumming behind his powerful eyes: *we gotta go in we gotta go in we gotta go in...* "Tash, they're gonna make us if we don't go in. This is it, don't you get it? This is the one."

"I know, Billy. I know that." Her heart is racing, Adrenaline is flowing. *We gotta go in we gotta go in.* Her instincts, as usual, are in sync with his. Except for one. "I just, I think we need to think about the —"

He brings his face close to hers. She smells the peppermint gum that she made him start chewing because she hated the smell of tooty-fruity. "Tasha, listen to me. There's just the two of them, that's it, just the two of them. She got her paycheck, so that means he's been using, he won't even put up a fight. But we've gotta do this. We nail him, just the two of us, and we're there. No more double shifts, no more bullshit from Crocker or Wagner.

Front of the class. Write our own ticket. But we have to go. Now."

She knows he's right. She can see it too, their starry future emblazoned in her mind. Billy's face is still inches from hers, urgent and smooth and not to be denied. The small voice of warning inside her is no match for him.

She looks at him, her eyes for once imploring. "Stick next to me?"

He beams. "Right behind you, all the way."

They share a hurried, horny kiss, and leap from the vehicle, charging toward the house.

But the image of that horrible crack row house rising up out of the darkness, closer and closer, began to fade, and suddenly other sensations intruded.

Words in her ears. "...can't die... You can't die..."

Convulsive spasms in her stomach.

"You can't... You gotta get it out..."

A hand in her mouth. Fingers down her throat. The nasty, bitter taste of bile.

"Come on, that's it, that's it..."

She retched again, the spasms reverberating through her body, drawing wails of protest from her already-spent muscles. Her eyes dimly registered the sight of half-digested pills a massive puddle of yellow-brown vomit, and of the person who struggled to hold her head steady as she poked a finger to the back of Natasha's throat once more.

"Don't die, Miss Briggs. Don't die, please..."

Andy.

THE LAST DAY

McGann surveyed the wreckage of Lincoln Meyers' garage.

It looked no better, yielded no more secrets in the light of day than it had the previous night. The fire department had saved the rest of the house, but the garage was a soggy, blackened shell. They had a witness, a neighbor who heard the explosion and the screaming, looked out his window to see Briggs jumping in her truck and driving away like the devil was after her. And then, what they found at Briggs' house.

What the goddamn hell is happening here?

He needed to get out of here, think this through, stop staring at the crime scene like some gawky housewife.

His phone warbled. The screen read: RANDOLPH. He stifled an urge to smash the phone to pieces and answered. "Yes?"

"Well?"

"We're working it."

"And?"

"We're working it."

"I'm not sure I like your tone of voice, Chief."

McGann felt the muscles twitch in the hand that held

the phone. He had to consciously still them in order to keep the hand from crushing the phone in its grip.

"I'm handling it, sir. We're—"

"I'm sending Joey to help you spin it."

"I don't think we need —"

"He'll be down there in an hour. Can you keep it together until then?"

"I... yes. Sir."

The call went dead. He shoved the phone in a pocket. "Fucker," he muttered. "Fucker."

"Sir?" McGann turned, startled. It was Dudley, his pudgy frame making a comical attempt at standing at-the-ready. McGann found he was already regretting putting Dudley in charge of the investigation, however few the choices. The man was at his most useless when he went into tin-soldier mode.

He wondered how much Dudley had heard, and glowered in annoyance. "What?"

"I... checked in with patrol, sir."

"By cell phone?"

"Yes, sir." He relaxed just a touch; Dudley had that much sense, at least. A radio call on the police band would have been caught by Merriman and God knew who else. "Still no sign of Briggs."

He fixed his iron gaze at Dudley. "I want her found. Do you understand, Dudley? I want her found now."

Dudley gulped. It caused his slight double-chin to wiggle. "I'm...on it, sir."

From behind him, he heard, "Chief McGann?"

He turned. It was Merriman, no surprise, leaning over the police tape twenty feet away, recorder at the ready. "Nothing more to report, Merriman."

"Just wondering if you can comment as to why Detective Briggs isn't leading the investigation." Damn the little weasel, he was no fool. Last night, Merriman had somehow gotten here even before the fire trucks.

"Detective Briggs is... working another case."

9:13

Behind Merriman, McGann could see two news vans pulling up.

Shit.

It was going to be a long day.

Natasha opened her eyes.

The room was dim and the air felt cool and stuffy. She shifted and felt every one of her muscles protest, her body a knot of pain and exhaustion. She touched her face and felt a sheen of greasy sweat. She raised her head and propped it on an elbow, taking in more details – lumpy mattress, cheap polyester bedspread, worn furniture pocked with cigarette burns. She was in a motel room, and not one of the better ones.

Andy sat in the tattered armchair across from the bed, watching her with tired and doleful eyes. She whispered, "All I've ever done is lie to you."

Natasha tried to sit up, winced at the pain that roiled in her stomach. "And save my life. We're even."

Natasha glanced around for her phone, for a clock. Sensing the question, Andy said, "It's about twelve-thirty. You've been out a while." Then she added, "We're at the Sunspot Motel. On Highland Road toward Beckettsville. I… had a feeling I should get you out of there."

Andy's skittishness, her prickly defiance, were gone. Her voice was voice bent with emotion. "You try to run from your sins. But you can't ever run fast enough. I tried. I tried to put them behind me, but they come back. I can't ever escape, I can't ever get away. I've seen, Miss Briggs. I've seen."

Natasha sat up slowly, breathing through the vertigo as she perched on the edge of the bed, rested her feet on the floor. "Tell me, Andy. Tell me what you saw."

Andy told her.

Andy opens the kitchen door.

Crystal is there.

She's wearing a denim skirt and her flower-print tank top, the one she wears only on the rare occasions when the bruises on her back are totally faded. She's barefoot and her hair is down, and Andy's heart feels like a knot in her chest.

But something is wrong. Crystal paces the floor of the spotless kitchen, her expression frayed and distraught, her cell phone pressed to her ear. She does not acknowledge Andy and Andy is not surprised. This is a vision from the past, and any chance Andy might have had to be a part of it is long gone.

Andy suddenly realizes how strange it is that Crystal is talking on the phone. She can hold a conversation by text for hours, but she rarely calls anyone, and no one calls her.

Except… Except maybe for him.

Crystal asks, "What am I gonna do? What am I gonna do?" She speaks in the clipped, rapid-fire way she has when she is deeply upset. She is fighting back tears and losing, caught between anger and terror. Whatever the reply, it only upsets her more. "Figure something out? What the fuck are we supposed to figure out? Huh? Like what? What?"

She leans her elbow against the counter and rests her forehead in her hand. The phone comes away from her ear just long enough for Andy to hear the voice on the other end. It's a man's voice, trying to be comforting, conciliatory. But whatever the words are, they bring her no comfort. Crystal says, "You're not gonna do anything, are you?" Silence as the other speaks. "You said you'd take care of me." Her voice breaks into a ragged moan. "You said. You *said*."

For an instant, Andy hears the man's voice again. "Look… Crissy…"

But Crystal jabs the "end call" button. Her face flares with wrath and she raises the phone over her head as if to smash it. But the moment passes, and instead she places the phone, with deliberate care, on the nearby table. She shudders and weeps. "Fucking bastard," she mutters. "Fucker. You fucker!"

Andy feels her own tears on her cheeks. She remembers something from one of Bishop Pyle's sermons, "Only when the tears BURN your face, are you TRULY re-PENT-ant…"

Crystal wanders the kitchen, back and forth, her hands opening and closing and spinning pointless circles, a condemned woman awaiting the noose. Finally, exhausted, she slumps into a chair at the table. She notices the phone again, and her eyes brighten as if an idea, a shred of hope, has come to her. She picks up the phone, regards it as if it somehow might deliver her.

Andy knows what's coming.

Crystal begins to compose a text, but then seems to think better of it. Instead, she presses the "call" button and holds the phone to her ear. The call is not answered, as Andy knows it won't be. Voice mail kicks in. Crystal says, "Andy, Andy please –"

The hallway door bursts open.

Crystal and Andy cry out in unison.

Glen Salyers. He roils, ferocious and cold. Without a word, he closes the distance between himself and his daughter in one stride. He grabs her hair, bunched in his fist close to the scalp. He yanks her to her feet. She screams in pain and fear. With his other hand he jerks up her tank top to reveal the just-developing baby bump.

Crystal hitches back her cries, pants shallow breaths. "Daddy. *Daddy.*"

"Shut up!" He shakes her with the hand buried in her hair and she wails in pain. "You slut! You Goddamn slut!"

Crystal does struggle then, floundering against his unbreakable strength as he pulls her toward the kitchen door. She flails for something to slow her progress, grabs at a chair, at the door frame, shrieking in pain and terror. She is in the fight for her life and she knows it.

And she fails.

Glen barely has to break stride as he hauls her toward the basement door.

Andy finished her story and shook with dry sobs. Natasha handed her tissues and waited; she was still a cop and knew how to time a confession. When Andy's lamentations had dulled to whimpers, but before they disappeared completely, Natasha said softly, "Tell me what happened between you and Crystal."

Andy thought for a while, one hand absently caressing a fold of her skirt. "We were going to get jobs on cruise ships after we graduated, go around the world, party on every beach we stopped at. Then we'd move to California and work for the movie studios. She said she was going to do makeup, maybe even learn how to make monster faces and everything. I figured... hell, I didn't care. As long as I was with her."

"So what happened?"

Andy rested her head in her hand for a moment, and when she spoke again her voice was warped with grief. "Crystal was the kind of person who would get all excited about something, then she'd get bored and go on to something else. I just never figured she'd get bored of me."

Natasha felt the tingle that told her she was coming close, finally within reach of the truth, but the sorrow in Andy's voice made her wonder if it was worth the price. "I'm sorry. I know how you feel."

Andy suddenly looked up, her bloodshot eyes tight with suspicion. "Do you really mean that, ma'am? Do you really?"

Natasha could answer honestly. "I really do." After a moment, she asked, "Who did she ditch you for?"

The fold of skirt was now bunched in a pale fist. "She started hooking up with this guy. He wasn't our age. He was a lot older. Old enough to be her dad, I think."

Natasha felt a sick sense of understanding in the pit of her stomach. She knew where this would lead, but asked anyway, "Do you know the man's name?"

Andy shook her head. "She didn't tell me about it, but I got her phone when she wasn't looking. I saw a picture of him, read some of their texts." She took a breath, let it out slow and deliberate. "She caught me at it and started yelling, and I yelled back, and... after that, she was done with me."

Natasha said, "And then her father found out."

Andy nodded. "I'm the one who told him."

Natasha gasped. She couldn't help it.

Andy popped to her feet, began to roam the small room in agitation. "All I wanted, all I wanted was for someone to say... to be my friend and... and *mean* it. Was it so evil, was it so... *sinful* of me, to want that? I sent him an email. I figured he'd whip her, he'd make her break it up with that guy. Or maybe he'd beat the guy up and make him leave town. And then we... she and I... we could..." Suddenly spent, she dropped back into the chair, held her head in her hands. "I could have answered that call. I was right there. I could have answered it. She needed me, she needed me and I didn't answer, and you know what else? I *smiled*, Miss Briggs. I was signing her death sentence and I *smiled*."

Natasha rose. She wobbled, her balance still off, but she shuffled over to where Andy crouched and shuddered and laid a comforting hand on her shoulder. "You know that what he did wasn't your fault."

Andy didn't look at her. "I thought she ran away, like her dad said. I mean, why wouldn't she? After I turned my back..." She hitched a dry half-sob. "I made myself believe it, anyway. And then... and then Grace comes." She looked up at Natasha; her face trembled with the turmoil inside of her. "Don't you see? Don't you see, Miss Briggs, how I was punished? How God showed, showed his disfavor, how He brought my sins back to me?"

"Andy. Tell me about Grace."

Andy bowed her head again, her fingers suddenly still. "She was so scared, ma'am. She was so scared. She hadn't slept, she'd barely eaten anything the whole week. She was desperate, ma'am. Desperate. And I failed her, too."

Wait for it.

Andy continued. "I met with her. I prayed with her. I listened to her. She said, well, like I told you. A demon was attacking her. Every night. I was going to tell Bishop Pyle he should do the casting-out. I mean, maybe she was on something or maybe she was just crazy, but she was... sincere. I was going to do it. And then she showed me this."

From her nearby purse, she pulled out a folded piece of paper. It was weighty, high-quality paper, and Natasha remembered the artist's pad in Grace's desk. The drawing's subject came as no surprise.

Crystal.

Again Andy abruptly stood, and Natasha, caught off-guard, nearly lost her balance and had to kneel by the chair as Andy began once more to pace the small room. "I screamed at her. I told her to get out. What was I supposed to do? Just believe her? Believe her that, that Crystal, my dear Crystal..." Her outburst spent, she dropped onto the edge of the bed, hunched forward, a half-alive thing. "I've prayed," she said hoarsely. "I've made offerings of my pain. But God won't hear me. Twice He gave me the chance to practice His compassion, and twice I failed. There's no way, there's no way back from what I've done."

Natasha again reached out a hand to comfort her, but Andy flinched when that hand touched her back. It was then that Natasha noticed the blue-black bruises through the flimsy blouse.

Natasha shuffled to the chair and sat down, thoughtful. The pieces were coming together, finally. She doubted she would live past tonight, but perhaps she could at least solve one final puzzle. "Maybe you have another chance."

Andy looked up, her desolation momentarily yielding to surprise. "H-how?"

"You couldn't have saved Grace from Crystal even if you'd wanted to, but maybe you can help me."

"How?"

"First, tell me what Grace did, what she was sorry for."

Andy replied, "She was… hooking up with this guy, a redneck guy. She got pregnant."

Oh my God.

"She said her mom and her grandad said she had to… get rid of it."

Natasha thought hard. The facts touched but would not connect. She said aloud, "But the autopsy didn't…"

It was like an ice-cold hand touched her chest as the truth fell into place, larger and more dreadful than she could have imagined. Natasha asked, "You said you saw a picture of the man Crystal was seeing?"

"Yes, ma'am."

Natasha picked up her phone, found an image of Eddie Shifflett, and turned the screen toward Andy. She felt her throat begin to constrict as she asked, "Is that him?"

Andy blinked. "No, ma'am. The guy was older."

She'd already known it wouldn't be Eddie, but she had to try. She pulled up another photo and again showed Andy the screen. Andy considered the photo for only a moment before she said, "That's him."

It was a picture of Linc.

Andy must have read the understanding in her face, for she reached out a hand and closed it over hers. "Do you know, Miss Briggs? Do you know… why Crystal hurt Grace? Why she's hurting you?"

Natasha exhaled a long, quiet breath and faced the truth, the entire truth that she had avoided all these months. "Seven months ago, back in the city where I used to work, my partner and I went into a house when we shouldn't have, and a bad man killed my partner, and he hurt me very badly."

Andy was silent, curious.

Natasha said, "My partner and I were fu… we were having an affair."

"Yes, ma'am?"

"And I was pregnant."

After the story was finished, Natasha dozed for a while. Around two o'clock, she woke to find her appetite had returned with a vengeance. Andy brought back sandwich bread, peanut butter, and odds and ends from a nearby convenience store. Natasha ate, grateful that her stomach accepted the food. She found she was terribly thirsty and had to resist the urge to guzzle the bottled water that was part of the haul. She showered in a mildewed stall that smelled of bleach, luxuriated in the tepid water.

She found Andy back at her post in the easy chair, tearing apart a paper napkin, rolling the pieces into tiny balls. Natasha regarded the young woman, small and scared and lost in her misery. It wasn't actually that much of a jump from her to Grace Randolph, or to a hundred different girls she'd encountered in her career and in her life. It wasn't that much of a jump from Andy Wagner to her own self. Maybe that was the smallest jump of all.

Natasha said, "You really loved her, didn't you?"

"Yes," breathed Andy. "Yes."

Natasha sat down across from Andy on the edge of the bed. She was steady now; there was no longer any delay between her brain's instructions and her body's movements. "I'm going to need you to help me with something."

Andy asked, "What are you going to do?"

"What I should have done months ago."

Her phone read: 2:49.

This was the end for her, and she knew it. But before tonight, she had work to do.

Natasha dialed a number and was pleasantly surprised when the line picked up. A resonant voice said "Hello, this is Doctor Cummings."

"Murray, this is Detective Briggs. Don't hang up. It would be a very bad idea."

"Detective Briggs." She could hear his voice rise half an octave. "How can I... help you?"

"They told you not to talk to me, didn't they?"

"Well, Chief McGann –"

"You know, I wonder why he would think to warn you that I might be calling?"

"Well, I don't, I mean he –"

"Murray, I bet you only snarf candy when you're nervous."

"Detective, I really don't think I should –"

"I already know what you left out of Grace Randolph's autopsy. I know why you did it, and I know it's probably not the first time you've done McGann this kind of favor. I just want to hear it from you."

There was silence. For a moment, she thought he had fainted. Then he croaked, "If you, you think I'm going to sit here and, and admit, admit to –"

"You just did." She had to smile. There wouldn't be enough candy in the whole state to calm the poor guy down after this. "Now, Murray, why don't you get it off your chest?"

She dialed again, and the call picked up before the end of the first ring. "Briggs," said McGann, his tone cautious. "You need to come in and talk to me."

"You can do better than that, Chief. At least throw in that you need to 'find out what happened' or 'get my side of the story.'"

His voice hardened. "Briggs, you'll be lucky if all that happens is you lose your job."

"You know, Chief, I've been checking the news. Funny, there's a lot on right now about a police officer who died in a fire last night, but nothing about another police officer who broke into the house of the richest woman in three counties and pointed a gun in her face."

She had to smile at the discomfort in his reply. "She...decided not to press charges."

"Doesn't surprise me. She's afraid of the question I asked her, and so are you."

"What the hell are you talking about?"

"I had a chat with Murray. Turns out the poor guy has a conscience."

He floundered. "My God, you...you're out of your mind, you're –"

"I'll bet it would have looked really bad for Gerald Randolph if his granddaughter's autopsy showed evidence of a recent abortion." She could swear she heard the air going out of McGann's lungs. "I mean, he could have handled it with the voters, but not with the Family League, which were the ones who got him elected in the first place. Not too many people in this state who could pull off twisting a medical examiner's arm to alter an autopsy, but between you and Randolph, I bet you could do it."

Silence.

Got you.

"I'll bet," she continued, "that if I exhumed Glen Salyers' body, I'd find that the angle of the ligature marks was all wrong for someone who hanged himself."

9:13

McGann finally replied, "What do you want?"

A short, hollow bark of laughter rose from her. "What do I want? Do you think there's anything I'd ever want from Randolph, or from you?"

"You don't know what you're –"

"SHUT UP!" She felt it coursing through her, the hatred that had been her constant companion most of her life, and she reveled in it. "Crystal Salyers finally called the cops on her father, didn't she? She knew he was over the edge and she was finally going to press charges. And Linc was the responding officer, am I right? But he didn't arrest Glen, he didn't call social services, he called you. You! You said we take care of our own problems, and that's what you did. I'll bet that girl showed textbook signs of physical and emotional abuse and you left her to rot!"

"Detective." He tone was conciliatory now and it made her even angrier. "Detective, let's just meet and talk this through."

But she wasn't done. "But Linc, he's not as cold-blooded as you, and he's got a Prince Charming complex like nobody's business. Did you know about that? Did you know what kind of 'follow-up' he was doing on that case?"

Silence.

She forced her breathing to slow, her voice to calm. "Gerald Randolph was running for the state senate when Glen Salyers' body was found. I assume that's why you covered up what really happened. You and Linc found two other bodies in that basement besides Glen Salyers, didn't you? Where did you bury them?

A subtle, but sharp, intake of breath from the other end.

Got you again.

"Been a pleasure working with you." And she pressed the "end call" button.

She made another call, the last. This time, it went to voice mail. "Hi, this is Chad Merriman with the *Colvin County Times*. Please leave a detailed message and I will return your call as soon as possible." She waited through the sound of the beep.

"Hi, Merriman. I've got another scoop for you, and I bet this one could get you a desk at the *Times-Dispatch*, or maybe even the *Post* if you play it right."

She laid out the details as best she could in the time she had.

She hesitated, then, suddenly unsure of how to end the call. Finally, she said, "Merriman, I don't know if you actually cared or not, but you helped me and I thank you for that. Run with this story and get the hell out of the sticks while you can."

The door opened as she ended the call. Andy had come back from the shopping trip that Natasha had sent her on.

It was 4:37.

Suddenly there was time to kill, and Natasha couldn't think of a thing to do with it.

They ate again, tried and failed several times to make small talk, a skill it turned out neither of them had. Natasha settled on the bed, contemplating the cracks in the ceiling, dozing off and on, while Andy sat in the chair, equally silent.

When Natasha woke from her second or third doze, she found Andy with her eyes closed and her hands folded, her lips moving silently. Natasha shifted to the edge of the bed. "Are you praying?"

Andy opened her eyes. They were calmer than she'd ever seen them. "Do you pray, Miss Briggs?"

Natasha's eyes dropped. "He and I haven't spoken for a long time."

"Then pray with me."

9:13

Natasha closed her eyes, bowed her head, and listened as Andy gave voice to the words. They flowed into and around her. They surrounded her and immersed her. They did not touch her heart, for that was closed to Him and would remain so, but when the prayer was finished she felt closer to a sense of peace.

And then, "Amen," and it was over.

The clock on the nightstand read: 7:41.

Andy said, "I guess it's time to go."

Andy's car had no air conditioning, but for the first time all week the air felt cooler, the humidity less oppressive.

A good night to die.

Natasha chided herself for being dramatic, but the sentiment held true.

They were on a tiny, weeded-over track in the woods, with an impenetrable tangle of trees and brush on each side. Natasha asked, "You sure you know where you're going?"

"It used to be a logging road, but that was years before Mister Salyers bought the place." Andy was perched on the edge of the seat, peering into what seemed to Natasha to be complete darkness. "I memorized it so I could drive up to the back yard without the headlights on, so he wouldn't know Crystal was sneaking out."

Natasha cringed as Andy misjudged a curve and vegetation grazed the side of the car, a bunch of rough stems brushing her face through the window. "You still remember it?"

"Mostly." It was lucky they could approach the house from the rear, in case it was being watched, but Natasha doubted that Dudley was that smart. "You're sure you want to be part of this?"

"I'm sure."

The windshield seemed to light up in brilliant soft

blue as they emerged from the woods into the moonlight. Andy shut off the car, leaving them with the eerie silence of a country night. Andy asked, "Should I drive closer?"

"This is close enough."

She opened her door as Andy popped the trunk.

Andy leaned against the back porch rail and inhaled the quiet of the evening.

They were done with their work. The back porch on which they stood was shaded from the moonlight, but Andy could see the screen from Detective Briggs' phone. It read: 8:49. Andy watched as Natasha slipped the phone into her pocket, sending them back into gloom, and said, "It's time for you to go."

Andy tensed. "I should be here too, ma'am. I need to be here." Her voice caught. "This is all my fault, and I should be here."

But when Natasha answered, her tone had changed into something Andy hadn't heard from her before. It was soft and warm with compassion. "Andy, were you haunted last night? After you visited the house?"

Andy's brows knit in puzzlement. "No. I wasn't."

"Do you understand what that means?"

Andy shook her head.

A gentle hand touched her face in the dark. "It means she forgave you."

She could feel the realization, the wonderful truth of it, spread through her like a light. It was a combination of powerful joy and desolate sadness, but she smiled as she clutched Natasha's hand and pressed it to her cheek. "God bless you, Miss Briggs. Oh. God Bless you."

She felt Natasha's arms embrace her. "You're free, Andy. You're free."

The Salyers house was stygian and silent. The

9:13

stillness rested over Natasha like a blanket.

She sat on the kitchen floor to keep the glow of her smartphone screen from being seen from outside. The phone's clock read: 8:55, but that wasn't her concern at the moment.

She tapped an icon to open her photo file, finding and opening one in particular with practiced ease. It was a snapshot of her and Linc, taken years ago – *Christ, ten years almost* – at the police department picnic, her second year in Richmond and their fourth month on patrol together. Linc held a beer in his hand, she had a baseball bat over her shoulder, and they stood just a little too close, smiled just a little too brightly. A few hours after that picture was taken, they had made love for the first time.

She pulled up another image. It was an ultrasound, done at 8 weeks, and the fetus had just started looking like a baby instead of a tadpole. The baby seemed to be reaching for something just out of sight, reaching and wanting and alive.

Despite the heaviness in her heart as she beheld the photos, she felt a peace that she hadn't felt in a long time, maybe ever.

I'm free.
Tonight was the last night of her life.
I'm free.

The light from her phone was puny in its attempt to breach the blackness around her, but she felt her foot step from wood to concrete and knew she had made it to the basement. She turned off the phone and let the dark close in around her.

It was time.

"Crystal. I'm here."

And all at once, the light came on and the screaming started.

It was cold. The wood stove glowed. She saw Glen

Salyers, just as dreadful as she had envisioned him, his eyes shining with a sickening excitement. She heard Crystal scream, "Daddy! Daddy, help me! Please help me!" And one glance told Natasha everything, confirmed her most horrible suspicions.

Crystal lay on the concrete floor, the image of Natasha's nightmares – filthy, tattered, skeletal-thin. The chain was there, padlocked around her neck and secured to the metal ring bolted into the wall. The chain was about five feet long and would have given her just enough slack to reach the stinking bucket near the window or to add wood to the stove. Empty snack bar wrappers and water bottles, a filthy blanket and pillow, completed the terrible picture.

No one had looked for her. No one lived close enough to hear her scream for help. Crystal had been here for a long time.

She moaned again in agony. "Daddy. Help. Help."

Horror wrenched Natasha's heart as she beheld the reason for Crystal's cries. The girl was indeed pregnant, her belly mounded high. And her labor had begun.

Natasha fell to her knees. "Oh God," she wheezed. "Oh, God."

Crystal thrashed. She wailed in torment. Her fists pounded the concrete floor and the floor was spotted in blood.

Glen stood by and watched, unmoving. As Crystal's cries reached their crescendo, his face glowed with a kind of triumph.

Crystal emitted one final, desperate shriek.

There was a silence. The world took a collective breath to accompany a new life. But the silence was not broken.

The baby was dead.

Natasha vomited. The room was permeated by the smell of blood and shit. She trembled.

Crystal emitted a howl of grief. She cuddled the wet,

dead bundle against her chest and bleated in almost animal sadness. She could do little more. Her young body was long past its limits.

Glen stood over her. His triumph complete. "Are you sorry?"

Crystal looked up. She gasped, "Go to…. fucking…. hell." Natasha saw with amazement that the girl had never given in, through her imprisonment, beatings, near-starvation. She had never said she was sorry. And in her grimace of defiance, her hollow and brutish stare, Natasha realized the terrible toll Crystal's suffering had taken on her mind.

With military efficiency, Glen flicked open a pocket knife and cut the umbilical cord. In the next moment, he yanked the tiny corpse out of Crystal's arms.

"No!" Crystal shot out a stick-thin arm to stop him, which he swatted like a fly. "Daddy, stop. Stop!"

Glen rose. "Sinners must burn." He turned toward the wood stove.

Crystal shrieked, and Natasha shrieked with her.

Then, before Natasha's eyes, Crystal crossed the line into madness.

She roared, her face a mask of inhuman hatred. With a newfound, psychotic strength, she leaped to her feet, crossed the distance between herself and her father in a single bound, and wrapped the slack of the chain around his neck.

Taken by surprise, Glen fell, his head striking the stove with a wet *crack*. He struggled, yanking at the chain, flailing at his daughter with his fists, gurgling with fury, but his diminished strength was nothing in the face of Crystal's lunatic rage.

"Are you sorry!" she screamed. "Are you sorry! ARE YOU SORRY! ARE YOU SORRY!"

They thrashed amid Crystal's mad screams. Blood poured from the wound in Glen's head and anointed them both.

Then Glen was still. The blood flowing from the wound in his head slowed, then stopped. His expression was one of surprise as his face drained of color.

Crystal slumped against the wall, her father's lifeless body in her lap. A crimson stain bloomed across the floor in front of her. She was bleeding. She was dying.

She stared blankly into nothingness. "You will be sorry," she whispered. "You will be. You will be..."

She repeated the mantra again and again, until the very last of her life bled from her and her eyes closed for the last time.

Natasha closed her eyes, and wept.

Then, from behind her she heard, "Are you sorry?"

She again felt the cloying warmth of the basement in summer. The light was gone, but she rose and turned to face the voice in the darkness. Her eyes adjusted quickly. A tiny sliver of moonlight through the window helped her make out the ghost of Crystal Salyers. Its glower of hatred had not wavered, but it made no move against her.

Natasha regarded the specter without fear. "I know why you never said you were sorry. You weren't going to say it, no matter what. You weren't going to let him win."

The ghost was silent. There was no way to know if it had the power to think beyond its wrath, but she continued.

"A lot of people have come through this house since you died, and you've been here, you've seen into the souls of all of them. But you only punished Grace, and Linc, and me. Grace got an abortion. Linc turned his back on you and because he did, you and the baby you made together died. And I ran into that house in Richmond with no backup because I wanted to write my own ticket. And that was our sin, the same as your father's. It was our duty to protect our children, and each of us, in our own way, we abandoned that duty."

Her words, her heart, were heavy with remorse. "I

hated my father. I hated him so much that I never saw the ways I was just like him. I didn't see it until it was too late. All I had to do that night was put my child ahead of myself, but I didn't."

The ghost whispered, "Sinners must burn."

But Natasha wasn't finished. "And all you had to do was say you were sorry, and you might have saved your own child."

The ghost said nothing. Natasha had not expected a reply.

"There's probably not enough of you left to think about that. You refused to give in to him, and in doing so you became just like him."

Natasha pulled a lighter from her pocket.

"My baby didn't deserve to die. Neither did yours, or Grace's. Or you."

Next to her in the darkness was a tall gas can.
"And neither did Grace, or Linc."

The gas can fell over with a hollow thud, already empty, just like the three others upstairs that she and Andy had used to douse the house.

Gasoline dripped from the basement stairs.

Natasha said, "You haven't attacked anyone else in town, so that means you can't leave this house. People have to come here, first. And I will be the last person to come here."

She flicked open the lighter.
"I know I'll never leave this house again. And neither will you."

She tossed the lighter, flaming, toward the stairs.

It was too late to save the house, and that suited fireman apprentice Chase Dempsey just fine.

He'd only joined the VFD in the first place to score some much-needed points with the judge, after his second possession charge. Now he was stuck sweating like a hog in heavy firefighter gear, standing with old Ben McCluskey on the east side of the house and watching for flying embers. Once the tall grass around the house had been wet down, most of the crew had gone back to the trucks to pass the time. Some had even been allowed to go home. But McCluskey, who'd been in the VFD since before cell phones, was his official mentor, and McCluskey always went above and beyond. The old guy stood there like the pounds of heavy gear weren't killing him and the smoke and fumes weren't choking him, watching sharp-eyed for the smallest orange flicker to detach itself from the house. Chase longed for a cigarette and willed the house to burn faster.

The house seemed to obey his unspoken command.

The windows burst and flames lapped the siding like thirsty tongues. The blaze emerged through the roof, crowning the house in undulating flame. In the dark of night, the ugly, red-orange glow could probably be seen for miles. He had to admit it was exciting, in a way, though he'd surely miss the dead house parties. He snickered at the thought, *the dead house is dead*, but a glare from McCluskey cut him off.

Suddenly he said, "What was that?"

McCluskey turned his head. *Damn, the guy's not even sweating.* "What's what?"

Chase listened. He strained to hear above the rumble of the fire. "I thought I heard something. Like a...scream."

McCluskey turned his attention back toward the house. "Might have been hot air whistling through a pipe or something."

"You don't think anyone was in there?"

"If they were, they'd be dead 'fore we got here."

That seemed to settle it, but not for Chase. As the house continued to blaze, he listened again for the sound. *Pipes whistling? No fucking way.*

It was a scream, he was sure of it, not a scream of

fear or of pain, either, but of anger, of terrible rage. A scream that would have come out of the devil himself.

But he didn't hear it again. He stood and sweated and watched as hellfire consumed the house.

EPILOGUE

The wind was blowing the right way today, allowing her car radio to pick up a soft rock station out of Richmond that she liked. It was still morning and they were giving a news update. The panic over the "Virginia Torch Killer" was dying down. The Chief of the Wright's Crossing police department had been indicted for conspiring to alter two autopsies. Grace's grandfather had announced that he was going to run for governor. Andy only half-listened, finally shutting the radio off. It was a rare cool day in July, the humidity low enough to make keeping the windows down a pleasure. The breeze dispersed the smell of Edna Crowther that had clung to her.

She turned into the driveway of the Salyers house.

The house was gone, of course. The fire had consumed it completely. After Natasha Briggs' body was recovered, the city had filled in the basement with dirt. The police had patrolled the road regularly in the month after the fire to keep the freaks and partiers away. But now, in the light of day, there was no one to be seen. Andy shut off the car and breathed the stillness of the country morning.

9:13

She was different than the woman who had helped destroy the house that night. The bruises on her back were faded and there would be no more of them. Her clothes were still plain, but she stood straighter in them than before. The air tasted warm and alive to her.

From the back of the car she removed several trays of flowers in soil. She hadn't paid attention to the names, only picked the ones that were brightly colored, blues and reds and yellows, different hues splashed together to form a wild and beautiful whole. The ones that most made her think of Crystal.

The foundation still stuck out here and there, forming an intermittent perimeter around a large square of red Virginia fill dirt. She knelt at the far right corner and dug a hollow in the dirt, planting the flowers, covering them with potting soil, cracking the seal on a bottle of water so she could water them. Perhaps, as time went on, she could plant more, turn the entire sad grave into something that shouted with life. Dusting off her hands, she kicked off her flip-flops and walked toward the oak tree, delighting in the warm touch of the grass against her feet.

She knelt under the tree, closed her eyes and listened to the rustling of the leaves in the breeze. Maybe Crystal was buried somewhere nearby, her and the baby, or maybe they were far away. It didn't matter. The body was a meaningless thing next to the soul, and she bowed her head and prayed that Crystal had finally found her way to the place of eternal joy.

With a smile of hope, she prayed for all of them, for Crystal and her child, for Grace Randolph.

For Natasha Briggs.

The End.

ACKNOWLEDGEMENTS

This book has been in the making since the summer of 2006, when I first sketched out the idea for a screenplay about a troubled police detective who is haunted after investigating a death scene. A whole lot of people have helped get it from there to here, and my heartfelt gratitude goes out to you all.

To David Stewart, for inviting me on the cave trip that gave me the first spark of inspiration for the story.

To Sean Davis, for the notes that helped me sharpen the story into the screenplay that eventually became this book.

To the members of the Charlottesville Area Organization of Screenwriters (CAOS), who endured the endless drafts of the screenplay (and then a draft of the novel) and gave invaluable feedback every time. Special mention goes to Steve Zawacki, Pam Rodeheaver, and Doug Bari.

To Detective Jon McKay of the Albemarle County Police Department, for your thorough and helpful answers to my endless questions about police procedure. Thanks also in this regard to Master Officer Marcus Baggett, and to Kelly Hobbs.

To my brother, Jonathan Garrett, CRNA, MSN, for answering my macabre questions about severe burns, broken bones, and suicide methods. I knew I was on the right track with this book when you replied to one of my inquiries with, "At the risk of sounding like mom, don't the people in your books ever do anything nice?"

And, as always, to my wife Cindy, for the tough-loving edits and unflagging love and support you have given me over the years. You are my love and my inspiration.

ABOUT THE AUTHOR

Carl Garrett is the winner of the 2010 Austin Film Festival Screenwriting Contest in the sci-fi/horror category. His 9:13 screenplay was a finalist at the Shriekfest Film Festival screenwriting contest in 2012. He lives in Virginia with his wife.

Carl's short story, "The Zombie Town Bash," can be found at www.amazon.com

Connect with Carl online at ww.carlgarrettauthor.com

You can find him on Facebook at
https://www.facebook.com/Carl-Garrett-1395283854027406/?ref=bookmarks

You can email him at carlgarrettauthor@gmail.com

Made in the USA
Columbia, SC
09 June 2017